RESCUE A TALL TEXAN

Six members of the Pronto gang made a bad mistake when they kidnapped Stretch Emerson. The other Texas trouble-shooter, hard-boiled Larry Valentine, was soon free of the King County Jail, well armed, well mounted, and hot on their trail.

The Pinkerton agency and an Alvarado posse get into the action, but Larry is first to reach the secret hideout of thirteen homicidal outlaws, backed by the valiant Emma Dane and Slow Wolf, an old half-bred sidekick. It is there in that hideout that the Pronto gang face their final fatal showdown.

Rescue a Tall Texan

MARSHALL GROVER

A Black Horse Western

ROBERT HALE · LONDON

First published in Great Britain 1989

ISBN 0 7090 3740 6

Robert Hale Limited
Clerkenwell House
Clerkenwell Green
London EC1R 0HT

Photoset in North Wales by
Derek Doyle & Associates, Mold, Clwyd.
Printed in Great Britain by
WBC Print Ltd., Barton Manor, Bristol.
Bound by WBC Bookbinders Limited.

ONE

Dangerous Strangers

'I've had enough,' declared Robbie Bolger, the ageing but still active medico of King County. In disgust, he donned his derby. 'Nothing fouls up a good poker party like a sore loser, especially when he can't handle his booze.'

'I'm with you, Doc,' said Alec Hood, a local merchant.

'Me too,' growled horse-trader Ed Rynan. 'No fun in this game no more.'

'Gents,' said Larry Valentine, 'I sure agree with you.'

The game had begun around 8 pm. The clock above the shelves of the bar of the Golden Slipper Saloon now showed a quarter before midnight. Late winter cold was lingering in south-east Nevada and the saloon's stove provided inadequate heating. The saloon-keeper had retired forty-five minutes before.

The taller of the notorious Lone Star Drifters, Larry's partner, was oblivious to the chill in the atmosphere, much of which was concentrated around the poker table. He dozed on four chairs set in a line by the bar-room's south wall. And the other men present, six strangers occupying two tables near the batwings, had been studying the sleeper for the past hour and conversing in muttered undertones.

Mort Purnell, a heavy-set local in town suit and Stetson, was the reason the poker party was breaking up. Larry of the dark hair, rugged features and muscular six feet three frame had been a consistent winner simply because he was a wilier and luckier gambler. Purnell was the heavy loser, simply because he was inept at the game and had imbibed too freely.

These were all the parties present, except for the dispenser of cheer dozing on his stool behind the bar.

As the other players rose, Purnell rose with them, his eyes bloodshot, his expression ugly; he was focusing on Larry.

'You and your wild luck, smart-ass,' he jeered. 'How much luck, I'm wonderin', and how much ...?'

'Don't say it again, feller,' cautioned Larry. 'It'd make three times you hinted I cheat, and the third time could be mighty unlucky for you.'

'The game was square, nobody sharped anybody,' insisted Hood, and Rynan nodded agreement.

'Of course the game was square,' Doc Bolger said impatiently. 'Our burly friend's no cheat, Purnell, and if you weren't so drunk you'd realize it and take your losses like a true sporting man.'

Hood and Rynan nodded so-long to Larry and the medico and left. Stretch slumbered on, the six strangers still watching. The medico was about to say goodnight to Larry when, clear along Kingsville's main street, they heard an urgent drumming of hooves. One rider reined up in front of the Golden Slipper, swung down and, seconds later, came hustling in. He was young. King County was cattle country and he a hired hand of one of its biggest spreads, Bar Q.

'Hoped I'd find you here, Doc!' he panted. 'You're needed out to the ranch! Boss sent me to fetch you!'

'Damn and blast,' scowled Bolger. 'And me planning on being in my warm bed ten minutes from now.'

'It's the boss's wife,' said the cowhand. 'She's real poorly.'

The doctor turned to leave, but paused. Purnell was ranting at Larry, who pocketed his wallet and contemptuously turned his back on him. Then Purnell's temper flared. Out of control, he struck at Larry from behind, his fist bouncing off the side of his head. Larry reeled a couple of paces, cursed, whirled and swung a mighty uppercut. Purnell took it on the point of his chin, hurtled all the way to the bar, struck it with an impact that jerked the barkeep awake, then slumped to a squatting posture with blood trickling from his mouth.

In keen approval, Bolger remarked, 'Exactly what he deserved.'

'We gotta hurry, Doc,' pleaded the cowhand.

'Coming,' said Bolger.

Stretch was awake now, blinking at his partner, who grimaced irritably and blew on his knuckles.

'Runt ...?' he began.

'Nothin',' shrugged Larry. 'Damn fool clobbered me – and me with my back turned. He had it comin'.'

Stretch was about to resume his prone position when the patrolling deputy sheriff entered, hefting a shotgun. He was lean and beady-eyed and the beady eyes at once settled on the semi-conscious Purnell.

'What the hell happened here?' he demanded.

One of the six strangers, a scrawny, sharp-featured man in wool-lined jacket and beaver hat, drawled an apology.

'Sorry, my friends and me were talking business. Everything happened so fast, we just didn't catch the action.'

'Billy?' challenged the deputy.

'No use askin' me, Gilvray,' yawned the barkeep. 'I didn't rouse till Purnell hit the bar.'

Deputy Clay Gilvray cocked his shotgun and aimed it at the heftier of the tall men, at the same time darting a glance at the half-prone Stretch. Had Stretch been upright, his formidable height would have impressed Gilvray. Even bootless, the aptly nicknamed Woodville Emerson stood six and a half feet, revealed as a gangling, homely Texan with jug-handle ears and a Colt holstered at either hip. Like his sidekick of many years, he wore the rig of a range-rider.

Larry blew on his knuckles again and reprimanded Gilvray.

'Careful how you point that cannon, Deputy.'

'Don't give me no orders,' retorted Gilvray. 'Was it you downed Morty?'

'If you mean that bum …' Larry jerked a thumb, 'damn right I did. He was beggin' for it.'

'Is zat so?' scowled Gilvray. 'Well, the hell with you, whoever you are. I'm takin' you in for assaultin' an officer of the law. Now you unstrap your iron and pass it to me careful, hear?'

'That no-account's a lawman?' Stretch asked

incredulously, getting to his feet.

'Stay out of it, *amigo*,' ordered Larry. He glanced at the still-groggy Purnell, then at Gilvray. 'His coat's buttoned. How was I supposed to know ...?'

'Morty's a deputy like me,' declared Gilvray. 'Sheriff Appleby always says ignorance ain't no excuse, and that's good enough for me. You're under arrest.'

'Hell, runt ...' protested Stretch.

'You just take it easy,' soothed Larry. 'Plain enough it's no use talkin' self-defence to this badge-toter. Meanwhile, our horses're bedded snug in that stable along from the hotel we checked into. No sense wastin' that second bed. One of us might's well use it. Don't worry about it. I won't be in jail long.'

'That's what *you* think,' muttered Gilvray, as Larry surrendered his belted Colt.

'That's *just* what I think,' nodded Larry.

After Gilvray took Larry out, Purnell made it to his feet and stumbled after them, mumbling, mopping at his bloody mouth. Stretch shrugged helplessly, and the man in the beaver hat remarked in a friendly way, 'Lousy break for your buddy. Sorry we couldn't help.'

'I wish I'd been wide awake,' grouched Stretch.

'Texan, ain't you?' asked another of the six, a double-chinned character with a button nose. 'My friends and me never met a Texan we didn't like. How about a nightcap – on us?'

The man in the beaver hat went to the bar for a seventh glass. Deciding he could use a last shot before turning in, the taller Texan joined the strangers. He thanked them in advance and looked them over, all but the one filling a glass for him, so it was all too easy; he was unaware his whiskey was being spiked.

'My partner don't clobber *any* man,' he complained as he raised his glass. 'Not 'less some hothead's tryin' to clobber *him*.'

'Too bad we weren't payin' attention,' said another man. 'Else we could've talked up for your buddy.'

Stretch drained his glass, grunted his thanks and rose to leave. He stifled a yawn. Suddenly he was weary, wearier than he had felt in years.

For some time thereafter, he was only dimly conscious of what was happening, his companions offering to walk him to the hotel, his steps dragging when they finally reached the lobby of Sorley's Hotel, the sleepy night-clerk offering a key, the laborious climb to the double room into which he and his partner had checked mid-afternoon of the day before, one of his companions opening the door for him, he unstrapping his matched .45s as he lurched toward a bed – then nothing.

It was 8.45 am when, in bad humour, Dr Robbie Bolger returned to the county seat. At this time, Larry had just finished the indifferent breakfast served him in his cell and was assuring himself he would soon be free again. Before going to sleep, he had remembered one local, one witness who would support his claim of self-defence, the right to retaliate and his ignorance of his assailant's official status hereabouts. Just a matter of time, he assured himself.

The medico, hungry and disgruntled, dismounted upon reaching Dugan's Diner on North Main, tethered his horse and trudged in to seat himself at the table occupied by the coffee-swigging Deputy Gilvray, a mite bleary-eyed after working the graveyard shift.

Dugan delivered a platter of ham and eggs and Bolger began eating and, between mouthfuls, bitterly complaining.

'That damn jackass Hank Quinn!' he fumed.

'Talk soft, Doc,' warned the deputy. 'Quinn's gettin' to be a mighty important man, richest rancher in the territory.'

'I don't care how fat his bankroll is nor how big his herd,' scowled Bolger. 'He's over-protective of that fool wife of his, so, in my book, that makes him a jackass. And she's worse, a fool of a woman!'

'Easy,' soothed Gilvray.

'Easy be damned,' mumbled Bolger. He munched and swallowed and aired his grievance. 'Heart attack, Quinn insisted. Heart attack my ass. Annie Quinn's a glutton who eats too fast, always has, can't wait to properly masticate her food as any sensible woman does, so of course she's assailed by chronic indigestion, of course she has pain. Can you believe this? Quinn insisted I sit by her bed till sunrise! Well, by Julius, that's gonna cost him. I'll teach him to keep me out half the night, catnapping instead of getting my regular sleep. Wait till he gets my bill. It'll make his eyes pop!'

'Rough night for you, Doc.' Gilvray drained his cup and began building a cigarette. 'Mighty important night for me.'

'I didn't notice before,' said Bolger. 'But now I note you look remarkably smug this morning.'

'I got the drop on one of them hot-shot

trouble-shooters, arrested him, damned if I didn't,' bragged Gilvray. 'You know who I mean. Heard of Valentine and Emerson, huh?'

'For years,' nodded Bolger. 'And yesterday evening I finally met them.'

'This'll give Lucas Appleby somethin' to fret about,' gloated Gilvray. 'He knows I aim to stand against him at the next election, and what I did last night could swing the vote my way. The citizens're gonna remember it was me took the almighty Larry Valentine – and there wasn't a thing Emerson could do about it. I had my shotgun cocked. It would've pleasured me to blast 'em both.'

Bolger downed his last mouthful, took a sip of coffee and eyed him curiously.

'You arrested Valentine? What's the charge?'

'Assault on a law officer,' grinned Gilvray. 'I got to admit he's some hard hitter, that Valentine. Morty's head didn't clear till a half-hour later. He's missin' a tooth too. Oh, sure. I got Valentine cold.'

The medico turned red. He drained his cup, burped, rose and dropped money on the table while Gilvray surveyed him warily.

'Clay Gilvray, *you're* a jackass!'

'You're callin' everybody a jackass this mornin',' complained Gilvray. 'What the hell ...?'

'It didn't cross your mean little mind to question other parties present – witnesses to the incident?' raged Bolger. 'I remember Emerson was asleep, Billy too, but there were at least six other men in the bar-room who must've seen what I saw, young Toomey from Bar Q also!'

'What ...?' began Gilvray.

'Damn!' gasped Bolger, picking up his little black bag, donning his derby. 'Of all the bone-headed stupidity!'

He hurried out, slipped his rein, remounted and hustled his horse downtown to the office fronting the King County Jail. When he entered, the overweight Sheriff Lucas Appleby was seated in his desk chair, adjusting his spectacles, about to read official correspondence. The jailer lounged in the open jailhouse doorway.

The medico glared at Appleby and called him a jackass.

'Somethin' wrong, Doc?' frowned Appleby.

Bolger crossed the office, barged past the jailer, moved to the occupied cell, traded nods with Larry and assured him he'd have him out of here in just a few minutes. He returned to the office, stood arms akimbo before Appleby's desk and gave vent to his wrath. The jailer gawked and Appleby cringed as Bolger informed him of Deputy Purnell's ungentlemanly behaviour, his ineptitude as a card player, his too-heavy drinking and, worst of all, his whining, the whining of a sore loser. Appleby tried to get a word in edgewise.

'Sure, Doc, but ...'

'Shut up and *listen* to me!' snapped Bolger. 'As if that wasn't enough to break up the game – yes – we all quit in disgust – he three times cast aspersions on Valentine's integrity. That was unforgivable, Appleby. Men of Valentine's calibre never cheat at cards!'

'That didn't give Valentine any right to ...'

'I said listen, you bonehead! It was cold. Purnell's coat was buttoned, concealing his badge, and at no time did Alec nor Ed nor anybody address Purnell by his title of Deputy – probably because we don't consider him worthy of it. There was no way Valentine could know he was a lawman. And now comes the clincher. Purnell struck Valentine – from behind. Only then did Valentine finally give the bum what he'd been begging for all night. That, in case you've forgotten, is called self-defence!'

'The other customers ...'

'The hell with the other customers! I'm telling you what *I* saw! It happened just before I left to ride out to Bar Q!'

'Well now, Doc ...' began Appleby.

'Now you have the facts,' Bolger said grimly. 'So it's your duty to release Valentine immediately. You want to argue with me, Appleby?' He planted both hands on the desk and glared threateningly. 'If you had a brain in your head, you'd fire Purnell. And, by Julius, I've just remembered something. How could I forget? I've not yet billed you for attending Mrs Appleby during the week and a half she was bedridden with severe influenza. Your wife's in excellent health now.'

'Ruth's fine now,' nodded Appleby. 'And we sure appreciate ...'

'*She's* in excellent health.' Bolger bared his teeth. 'Wish I could say the same for your bank balance when I get around to tallying the bill. Let's see now. The daily visits to her bedside, the medicines, my services, my time ...'

'Your word's good enough for me, Doc!' gasped Appleby. He gestured frantically to the jailer. 'Don't just stand there, Toddy. Turn Mister Valentine loose, fetch his wallet from the safe, return his sidearm – hustle!'

Two minutes later, Larry was trading grins with the medico on the sidewalk out front, strapping on his Colt, thonging the holster down.

'Never was worried, Doc,' he said. 'Knew you'd be along to straighten things out.'

'Damn outrageous you spent the night in jail,' grouched Bolger. 'I'd have ordered your release – in fact you'd never have been arrested – if I'd still been in town when Gilvray made his show-off play.'

'Much obliged just the same,' Larry said as they shook hands. 'Doctors never can tell when they'll be called out. I know how it is.'

They parted then and, unhurriedly, Larry made his way to the Sorley Hotel. The day-clerk greeted him amiably, but shook his head to Larry's request for the key to Room 6.

'Must be in the room,' he said.

'You mean my partner ain't been down?' asked Larry.

'Haven't seen him,' said the clerk.

'Ain't like him to miss breakfast,' Larry remarked after checking his watch. 'By now, his belly must be growlin' up a storm.'

He climbed the stairs, approached the door numbered '6' and noted the key was in the lock. He tried the knob. It turned easily, much to his disapproval.

'Careless, careless,' he reflected as he opened the door. 'Beanpole, you're slippin'.'

Moving in, he closed the door behind him, glanced about and felt a slight chill not caused by the low temperature, though the window was wide open. Both beds were still made up, the nearest one showing an impression, an indication

Stretch had flopped on it diagonally. His and his partner's gear, their saddlebags, packrolls and sheathed Winchesters, were still in the corner. What increased the chill in his belly was the sight of a familiar buscadero shellbelt, double-holstered, with the holsters still full of Colt .45, on the floor beside the nearest bed.

He crossed to the window and climbed through to the gallery to stare down into the side alley. Firestairs led up to the gallery. Re-entering the room, he closed and locked the window. He took time to roll and light a cigarette – much needed – before quitting the room and locking the door.

When he descended to the lobby and gave the clerk the key, he asked as calmly as he could manage, 'You here when my friend came in last night? It would've been around midnight. No, likely a little later.'

'Didn't see him,' said the clerk. 'Dan Thayer, he's the midnight to six-thirty clerk this week and always punctual. Took over from me at midnight exactly.'

'Where'll I find him?'

'He lives at Mrs Gerald's boarding-house on Hoyt Road, next cross-street uptown.'

It took Larry only five minutes to find the boarding-house. Thayer's landlady, the matronly Josephine Gerald, protested he should not be disturbed.

'I don't wake him till eleven-thirty as a rule. Hotel clerks need their sleep.'

'And I'm real sorry about this, ma'am,' Larry said politely, but firmly. 'Got to talk to him just the same. It's an emergency, so I'd take it kindly if you'd show me to his room.'

After a little more persuasion, Mrs Gerald led him upstairs and knocked at a door until the sleeper roused.

'It's that time – already?' Larry heard the man grumble.

'No, Mister Thayer, but somebody has to talk to you,' she called. 'An emergency, he says.'

'Thank you, ma'am,' said Larry.

She withdrew after he opened the door. Thayer, a thin man, sat up blinking and tousle-haired as he crossed to the window to raise the shade.

'Aw, hell,' he grumbled. 'What emergency?'

'Ain't sure yet,' said Larry, perching on the side of the bed. 'Got some questions for you. Your head clear enough?'

'Well, I'll try,' said Thayer.

'My partner and me checked into Room Six yesterday,' said Larry. 'He's an uncommon tall hombre, six and half feet and homely.'

'*He's* uncommon tall?' frowned Thayer. 'Mister, *you're* no sawn-off.'

'Let's stay with my partner,' urged Larry. 'You were on duty when he came in after midnight, gave him his key?'

'He was bushed,' recalled Thayer. 'I don't believe he'd have made it upstairs if those other two weren't helping him.'

'What other two?'

'Strangers. I never saw 'em before.'

'Then they came down again?'

'I guess so. Got to admit – well – I was a little drowsy myself …'

'You could've been catnappin' when they came down.'

'Well, working the midnight to six-thirty shift,

we're entitled to a little ...'

'Okay, I ain't complainin'. But that's all you know? You didn't see anybody else, hear anything?'

Thayer shook his head. Larry thanked him, rose to lower the window-shade and invited him to go back to sleep.

By the time he reached the livery stable closest the Sorley Hotel, premonitions plagued him. He disciplined himself to stay cool and, with every passing minute, strove to resist his increasing apprehension. Nothing he had learned so far was typical of the easy-going tag-along who had followed him into and out of a hundred and one life-or-death crises not of their choosing.

For more years than they cared to recall, the nomads from the Lone Star State had sought peace and quiet, but in vain. It seemed they were destined to lock horns with the lawless everywhere they roamed. Peace and quiet had been denied them; they lived in the shadow of violence and the threat of sudden death and, for a wonder, had survived, always one jump ahead of their homicidal adversaries, always a shade faster with their fists and weapons, and accurate when it mattered most. Sometimes they had asked the obvious question – how long could their Lone Star luck last? And now the question bedevilled him again. Had that time come for his partner?

Moving into the stable, he made for the two end stalls. His horse, a rangy sorrel gelding, nickered at him. The stall beside the sorrel's was empty. Stretch's pinto wasn't there. On the rail supporting saddles, he saw his own, not his partner's.

The stablehand trudged in from the rear, a

bleary-eyed old-timer whose red nose suggested he was no teetotaller.

'Remember me?' challenged Larry.

'Yeah, sure.' The stablehand squatted on a box by the rear door. 'You and your buddy checked your critters in yesterday. Mornin', wasn't it? Might've been afternoon. I don't recollect exactly.'

'I guess you weren't awake after midnight,' said Larry.

'Well, on and off,' shrugged the stablehand. 'Not much business after midnight. It gets cold. Man needs a bottle, you know? Little somethin' to warm his innards?'

Larry forced himself to patience. If he hoped to learn something from this bottle-loving old-timer, bullying wouldn't do it. He would have to take it slow, coax it out of him. Stroking the sorrel's mane, he said steadily. 'I'm lookin' for my partner. You'd have to remember him. Likely the tallest hombre you ever saw.'

'Ain't forgot him,' nodded the stablehand. 'He sure is a tall'un.'

'I guess you must've been catchin' up on your sleep when he saddled up – you remember the pinto – and rode out,' Larry suggested.

'Mister, he was in no shape to ready his own animal,' declared the stablehand.

He talked and Larry listened. Yes, he had roused from slumber and remarked on the condition of the tall man dumped on the barn floor by two men who then set about saddling the pinto. One of them told him the sleeper was an old buddy of theirs. He had tied one on and would no doubt suffer the doozie of all hangovers when next he woke. They would take care of him. The stablehand asked about the other Texan. His inquisitiveness didn't seem to bother them.

'Waitin' outside, they said.'

'Uh-huh,' grunted Larry. 'Then what?'

'Said they were southbound,' recalled the stablehand.

'All right,' said Larry. 'What else did you see?'

'Wide awake by then,' said the stablehand. 'After they led the pinto out with your buddy roped ...'

'Roped?'

'So he couldn't fall off, I figured. Hands roped to his saddlehorn, feet tied into the stirrups?'

'You get curious again?'

'Well, I wouldn't know why they lied, but they sure ain't headed south.'

'How could you tell?'

'Watched 'em. Waited till they was clear of here, then I watched 'em head south along Main Street, but only as far as Cropper Street. Seven of 'em, includin' your buddy. *Couldn't* be southbound. They rode left into Cropper Street, wouldn't do that 'less they're headed east. There's a trail starts about fifty yards on from the east end of Cropper.'

'That all you can tell me?'

'All I know.'

'Okay.' Larry gave him a silver dollar. 'If you didn't get a clear look at 'em ...'

'Sorry,' said the stablehand, pocketing the coin. 'Night-time, just one lamp – and turned low at that – I don't see so good.'

'I'll be back for my horse,' said Larry, turning to leave.

He was working his memory while making for

the Golden Slipper, dimly recalling a half-dozen men present during last night's poker party but seemingly disinterested, keeping pretty much to themselves. The hell of it was he had paid little attention to them; when playing poker, he concentrated on his cards, letting nothing distract him. Now he suspected the six were more interested in Stretch anyway. By putting Purnell on the floor and running foul of the local law, he had let his partner down, failed him. A man doesn't treat a friend that way, the best friend he ever had.

Billy, the balding barkeep, was lethargically swabbing the bartop when Larry confronted him.

'Thirsty?' he asked.

'I could use a beer,' said Larry, dropping money on the bar. 'Draw one for yourself.'

'You're a gent don't like drinkin' alone,' Billy observed while filling a couple of tankards.

'Or travellin' alone,' muttered Larry.

'Hey, that must've been some punch you give Morty Purnell,' grinned Billy. 'Wish I'd seen it. Wasn't till he hit your side of the bar that I woke up.'

'How about earlier?' prodded Larry. 'What can you recall of six hombres that sat real quiet?' He jerked a thumb. 'Had a couple tables pushed together over there.'

'Oh, them?' Billy stroked his nose. 'They ain't from hereabouts. I never saw 'em before. Came in a little while after you and your friend. After the other deputy arrested you, they bought your friend a drink.'

He gave Larry as good a description of the strangers as he could manage, after which Larry bought a couple of bottles of good rye and made his next call, this time at the general store run by one of his companions of what had become a less than congenial poker party, thanks to the surly Deputy Purnell.

Alec Hood waited on him personally, filling his order, stowing the provisions in a sack. He paid the storekeeper and thought to ask about a pack-horse.

'The stable up from Sorley's rents ...' began Hood.

'I'll be buyin',' said Larry. 'Mightn't see Kingsville again.'

'Better do business with Ed then,' advised Hood. 'You remember Ed Rynan. He was in the game.'

'I remember him,' nodded Larry.

'At poker or selling a horse, Ed always deals square,' Hood assured him.

Following Hood's directions, Larry toted his provisions to Rynan's Square Deal Corral and chose and paid for a strong-backed dapple. Rynan threw in a rig, bridle and tie-rope and, within the quarter-hour, Larry was straddling his sorrel, his saddlebags, packroll and sheathed rifle slung, leading the pack-animal toward Cropper Street. Now the dapple wore Stretch's saddle and toted Stretch's gear, along with the provisions, by no means a heavy burden.

Pushing on from the east end of Cropper, he found the trail and the tracks of seven saddle-horses and wondered how long it would take, how many miles he would have to travel, to overtake six men who had kidnapped his partner.

That was the word – kidnapped. He had to accept the harsh fact that, for whatever their reason, six men had spirited Stretch out of Kingsville – and with ridiculous ease. The moment Gilvray took him out of the Golden Slipper, they had talked to Stretch. Everything friendly, Billy the barkeep recalled. And Stretch had fallen into a trap.

'He wouldn't get dead drunk just because he saw me arrested,' he assured himself. 'Wasn't drunk at all. One of 'em slipped somethin' in his whiskey – only way it could be done. They're sly, they're smart, and now they got him.'

Ransom? That possibility wasn't worthy of consideration. How much cash could they hope to collect from him for the safe return of his partner? His and Stretch's joint bankroll tallied to some $625 at this time. Split six ways, hardly worth the effort. No ransom note left in the hotel room anyway. So it wasn't ransom. They had another purpose.

He considered possibilities and mentally flinched. In their long war against the lawless, the Texas Trouble-Shooters had slain or captured many a badman, *too* many it now seemed. Outlaws have kin or friends. It had happened before, fathers, brothers or cousins seeking vengeance for the death or imprisonment of kinsmen who had been the losers in a clash with two drifting bandit-fighters of formidable reputation.

'They didn't want me,' he reflected. 'Just Stretch. And, when I clobbered that sonofabitch Purnell, I gave 'em their chance.'

He made a vow as he followed the tracks eastward. If they killed their captive, all six kidnappers would answer to him. And pay the supreme penalty.

TWO

The Merciless and the Doomed

At about the same time Larry Valentine rode out of King County, the nineteen-year-old known to the outlaws as the Reno Kid was spoiling for action.

'I didn't join up with the Pronto Gang just to help guard this secret camp,' he complained. 'Proved I got what it takes, didn't I? So I say it's high time the Boss got me ridin' with the outfit.'

The other man guarding the hideout high in the Sierra Solitario leered at the youngster and offered advice, his tone suggesting he didn't care either way. The Kid could heed or ignore this advice. No skin off Big Red Huber's nose.

'If you value your health, Kid, don't try hustlin' Jethro. He don't much appreciate young'uns' impatience. Liable to take a whip to you.'

The blond youngster waxed sullen, staring about him at the plank and tarpaper shacks and tattered tents ringing this high basin. High too were the slopes surrounding the secret camp, the inner ones timbered and rocky, the outer ones barely sloping at all, almost sheer rock walls. Great hideaway, he conceded. Well, wasn't this typical of Jethro Tragg, boss of the Pronto Gang, his personal hero? By golly, this place even boasted a secret entrance. Small wonder no search-party of lawmen, including Federal marshals, had ever gotten within ten miles of Tragg's roost.

He squatted by a fire with the hefty redhead, still airing his grievance.

'You got to admit I think fast.'

'Oh, sure,' drawled Huber. 'I'll allow you're fast with that purty iron you're packin' too. And it was smart and slick, the way you shook the Harper City posse off our backs. You made damn sure they couldn't tag us no farther'n the gorge.'

'Would any of you – includin' the Boss himself – have thought of settin' fire to that old bridge?' challenged the Kid. 'Lucky for you I was around.'

'It better be true what you told Jethro when you caught up with us,' warned Huber. 'If he finds out you lied, if there's any chance the posse recognized you ...'

'They were too far back,' the Kid assured him. 'Hell, you jaspers were only a hundred yards ahead when I crossed the bridge. Then all I had to do was gather a mess of dry brush, dump it on those dry planks and throw a match.'

'I'll allow the bridge was burnin' good by the time them Harper City chasers reached it,' said Huber. 'You shook 'em off and bought us some time, but you're still lucky you didn't get blowed right off of your fine black colt when you caught up with us and smart-talked Jethro.'

'Didn't smart-talk him,' the Kid said defensively. 'Just said as how he owed me and I hankered to join up with the outfit. He only had to look back to see all that smoke. He knew I did what I said I did.'

'Be thankful Jethro thought it was funny,'

advised Huber. 'If he wasn't feelin' so happy, after us lootin' the bank, he might've blasted you then and there.' He studied the Kid intently. 'For your sake, what you said about yourself better be true.'

'All true,' insisted the Kid.

'For sure?' frowned Huber. 'You're an orphan that don't belong any place, ain't nobody gonna miss you, try findin' you?'

'All true,' the Kid repeated. 'I was a loner till I threw in with this outfit, and that's what I always craved.' His eyes gleamed. 'To ride with the Pronto Gang.'

'There's harder ways for a man to get rich,' shrugged Huber. 'Meanwhile, bide your time, Kid, stay real patient and follow orders. You'll get to ride with a raidin' party when Jethro decides you're ready – and not before.'

The Kid rose and stretched. He looked younger than his nineteen years, a sturdily built, smooth-faced tearaway two inches under six feet tall. The Colt with its staghorn grips was slung to his right hip in a tied-down holster and, on appearances, he was what he claimed to be, a rebel with an itch for the outlaw trails.

'Which party'll get back first, d'you think?' he asked. 'The Boss's or Sid Werris's?'

'I calculate we'll see Sid before we see Jethro,' said Huber. 'Sid's bunch had a likely target, a bank at Cobbsburg, little town a ways south of Carson City. Jethro's hittin' a Butterworth stage up by the west Utah border. It'll take him longer to come home. He could get slowed down, might have to stake out and ambush a posse, somethin' like that. We've talked enough, Kid. You'd better get on up to the lookout post now.'

The ascent was no great effort for the Pronto Gang's newest recruit, and the youngest. As he turned toward the west slope, Huber voiced a hunch as to Jethro Tragg's main reason for adding the Kid to the band. Tragg was superstitious. Until the Kid joined them, the gang numbered thirteen.

Unhurriedly, the Kid climbed the west slope of the basin. From the high rocks on that side he would command a long view of the brush, high brush, and the timbered terrain penetrated by raiding-parties returning to base.

When he finished his climb, the Kid perched atop a high rock, rolled and lit a cigarette and assured himself this was the life, this was for him. He had long yearned to be part of a daring and elusive band of outlaws, and now he had made it.

It was night when Stretch came to his senses. He opened his eyes and, at once, questions plagued him. His head throbbed. The pain seemed to increase as he strove to get his brain working and his eyes focusing. Which night was this, he wondered? He didn't have to be a genius to realize he had been drugged. But how long ago?

He was huddled on his left side, ankles bound, hands tied behind him. After some blinking against the glow of the cookfire, he studied his captors. Six of them, and he had seen them before. Sure. The six in the saloon at Kingsville who had treated him to a nightcap after a deputy marched his partner to the local calaboose. Some nightcap. He had only a vague recollection of making it to the room at Sorley's Hotel and of unstrapping his Colts, but nothing after that.

A rogue with a knife-scarred chin glanced his way. Ivers was his name. He was eating, talking with his mouth full, but Stretch supposed his companeros were used to that.

'He's come to at last, Sid,' he mumbled.

'Sure? asked the man in the beaver hat.

'I'm sure,' nodded Ivers. 'He just opened his eyes. I wondered if he ever would.' He frowned at another man. 'Hell, Cy, you slipped *three* of them pills into his booze. Ain't that enough to kill a man?'

'Not enough to kill a famous trouble-shooter,' said Sid Werris, grinning across at the captive. 'What's the matter, Emerson? Cat got your tongue? Come on, your eyes're open, your mouth too.' Stretch tried to speak, but could not yet manage it; his mouth and throat were dry. 'Give him some coffee, Elmo. And load a plate for him.'

Broken-nosed, thick-lipped Elmo Stark filled a cup and bent beside Stretch to feed him a few gulps.

'Want me to untie his hands?' he asked.

'Not a chance,' said Werris. 'They're just full of tricks, Emerson and his sidekick.'

'I gotta feed him with a damn fork?' scowled Stark.

'He has to be good and healthy when we turn him over to Jethro,' insisted Werris. 'Won't be no fun for Jethro if he's weak and starvin', Elmo. Everything Jethro's gonna do to him – he has to *feel* it.'

Stretch swallowed and mumbled his first question.

'How long've I been out?'

'Quite a time, hot-shot,' said Werris. 'You left Kingsville with us a couple nights ago.'

'You're ours now, trouble-shooter,' muttered the

bushy-browed Farley Cross. 'And you can forget Valentine. No way he could take you away from us and, besides, he'll be stuck in the King County Jail a month or more.'

'Lawmen don't take kindly to saddlebums beatin' up lawmen,' taunted Werris.

'You're ours now,' repeated Cross. 'Till we're back where we hole up. Then you'll be Jethro's – all his for the killin'.'

Stark had loaded a plate. Now he hauled Stretch to a sitting position, his back against a tree, and began forking food into him. Stretch masticated and swallowed, secretly grateful he kept the food down. He kept on eating until Stark fed him the last forkful. Then he licked his lips and tried talking again; his speech was clear now.

'I'm tryin' to make sense of this. Seems like you hombres took a lot of trouble to find me in Kingsville ...'

'That was just luck,' said Werris. 'We're headed back to our roost. Took a bank a week and a half ago. Only stopped by Kingsville for supplies and to rest our animals – and there you were. So we just waited our chance, and your hothead buddy made it easy for us.'

'But we've always been keepin' our eyes peeled, hopin' to sight you and Valentine.' These words were lisped by a sallow, long-jawed rogue with close-set eyes, Pete Murquette. 'Jethro's orders. Wherever we are, every man in the outfit, we got to watch out for you big brave outlaw-fighters – but you specially, tall feller.'

'So Jethro's a boss-bandido totin' a grudge against me,' mused Stretch.

Scrawny Carl Ivers traded leers with the

hulking Cy Aberlain and remarked, 'He's finally catchin' on.'

'Helluva lot I don't catch onto,' complained Stretch. 'Jethro *who*? And what's his gripe against me?'

'Jethro Tragg,' growled Werris. 'The name Tragg don't mean anything to you, huh? And I bet you don't remember Jethro's brother Ruben either.' Stretch shook his head and wished he hadn't; the aching resumed. 'It's been a lot of years, but Jethro don't forget. Rube and some buddies of his held up a bank in Stockton, Utah, four years ago. You and Valentine arrived in that town just as they came out of the bank. There was a lot of shootin' and you hot-shots just had to get into the action, had to be heroes again. Only one of Rube's buddies got away – meanin' *me*. I saw Rube go down and it was you gunned him, Emerson.'

Stretch eyed him steadily.

'I guess it makes no difference to Tragg,' he said, 'that I only shoot at a man drawin' a bead on me. My partner and me, we ain't butchers, we just defend ourselves.'

'You're right,' chuckled Werris. 'It won't make no difference to Jethro. Ever since I told him what happened in Stockton, he's craved to get his hands on you, talked of how he's gonna make you pay.'

'Jethro still mourns Rube,' muttered Ivers. 'Just thinkin' about him makes him crazy. Hell, Emerson, I'd hate to be in your boots when he starts on you.'

'Believe this, hot-shot,' breathed Werris, spite flashing in his eyes. 'It won't happen fast for you. You think you know what pain is? Forget any pain you ever had. Jethro'll do it slow, likely it'll take a couple days, maybe three. He hungers to hear you wail, savvy? You have to *suffer*, he keeps sayin'.'

'And, while he's workin' me over, you heroes stand around and watch,' Stretch said contemptuously. 'Your idea of fun.'

The jibe cost him two savage back-handers and a kick to the ribs. Plainly, Werris was as much a sadist as his leader. He was wide-eyed, panting heavily, when Aberlain and Cross restrained him.

'Don't foul up everything, Sid,' soothed Aberlain. 'You're doin' fine so far.'

'Bound to get us a big handout from Jethro for bringin' Emerson to him,' said Cross. 'But you said it yourself. We deliver him half-dead, Jethro'd have to go off half-cocked. You want to risk that?'

'Trouble-shooters – big heroes – show-offs!' fumed Werris, returning to the fire. 'When I think of all the good men who'd still be ridin' free – but for this stinkin' reb and his sidekick ...!'

'Good men my ass,' Stretch mumbled, spitting blood.

'Shuddup, Emerson!' gasped Ivers, as Werris made to rise again. 'Just *shuddup* – 'less you crave more of the same!'

Later, when his captors bedded down, all but the one sitting guard in this grove south of the trail, Stretch closed his eyes, waited for his pain to ease and pondered his predicament.

'Bad one this time,' he reflected. 'You've got yourself in a bad mess; many a tight fix, but this beats all. They got you hogtied good and, wherever they're takin' you, there's worse trouble when you get there, some sonofabitch with a heavy chip on his shoulder and a cravin' to kill you slow. Oh, sure, this time you're sure as hell buzzard-bait – but not till the boss-man's through with you.'

He thought of his one hope, his compadre, Larry of the agile intellect, cunning, resourceful and, when needs be, every inch as ruthless as these outlaws, more so in fact. Larry *was* his only chance, but where was he now? Stuck in the King County calaboose and, as one of these bandidos had predicted, apt to be there a month or more.

But wait a minute now. His captors had been right there in the saloon, had seen everything, but had overlooked an important detail, specifically a witness who would surely demand Larry's release. Before dozing off, he had noted the less than congenial atmosphere prevailing at the poker table. The other players, one of them a local doctor, were resenting the jibes and thinly-veiled accusations mouthed by the sore loser. And when he was rousing from slumber, hadn't he heard the doctor's voice, maybe before he opened his eyes? What was it Doc Bolger had said about the jasper downed by Larry? He deserved what he got, something like that.

'Then the doc got called away,' he remembered. 'Well, okay, but he's got to come home to Kingsville *some* time, and when he does, when he finds out Larry got arrested by the other deputy – hey now!'

He would cling to that hope, the hope the medico would tell the truth of the incident to the county sheriff. And how long would it take Larry, free again, to figure out what had happened to his vanished partner? Not long at all. Why, at this very moment, Larry could be nightcamped somewhere west, resting in anticipation of resuming his bird-dogging chore come sun-up. There would be tracks for him to follow and he would follow them – stealthily. Heavy odds hadn't deterred Larry before and never would. So these bandidos had a secret hideout? No matter. Larry would find it, or maybe overtake this party long before its destination was reached.

Meanwhile, maybe the captive's luck would change. A chance might arise, an opening, an opportunity he would seize. He could forget about loosening his bonds; these bastards had knotted them tightly. But, if they dumped him against something sharp such as the edge of a broken rock, anything he could rub his ropes against long enough for them to fray. Yes, he would bide his time and wait his chances. All he needed was to get one hand free and empty the holster of the man nearest him.

It was something to dream about. He could sleep now, a prisoner, sure, but with his hope restored, his warrior instinct not exactly dormant.

Soon, Larry too would sleep. Frustration bedevilled him, but he resisted it as best he could; always the realist, he acknowledged he could achieve nothing by letting his emotions run riot.

He smoked his last cigarette before bedding down, hunkering by a fire built of wood carefully selected, slow-burning and giving maximum heat, minimum smoke. He cursed but acknowledged his need to keep safe distance between himself and the party he'd been following. Lonely country this, much of it wide open, much of it rock-littered, marked by straggles of brush and stands of timber. Low ground and high. From any of the high points along this route, a tag-rider could sight him if he carelessly travelled an unscreened section of the trail.

Not much wind. That was something. At least the hoofprints weren't fading. The tracks told him they were taking their time, obviously travelling familiar terrain and confident they would encounter no opposition. This disadvantaged him. He too had to travel slow. Only at night, and if it were dark enough, could he move at speed, and this had become his routine; he would be on the move long before sun-up.

At this stage, he wasn't counting on bird-dogging them all the way to their destination. They could be part of a sizeable owlhoot pack. His chances of rescuing his partner would be greater if he could find them nightcamped somewhere along their route. There would be a sentry – quickly silenced. Then, if he could reach and free his partner before the other kidnappers began stirring, he would have an edge; against five adversaries, he could wreak havoc with his Colt and Winchester.

He flicked the last inch and a half of his quirley into the fire and, as he rolled into his blanket, calculated the distance separating him from his quarry. A day and a half's riding, he decided.

An hour before sunrise, he downed a breakfast of beans and coffee. Then he was on the move again, straddling the sorrel, leading the dapple, heading back to the trail, and eastward again. Later, when the sun rose, he easily discerned the horse-tracks. As clear as yesterday. Seven saddle-animals, and still moving east.

There was a chill in the air, but the sunlight was bright and the faint wind blowing toward him when he sighted movement. Jack-rabbits, about a half-dozen of them and well in rifle range. As he unsheathed his Winchester, he had only two thoughts. One, the need to maintain his supply of fresh meat. Two, the direction of the wind giving his quarry little chance of hearing his shots.

He rose in his stirrups, took sight on one of the running jack-rabbits and squeezed the trigger. With the report, that critter – and another – abruptly stopped running. He reined up in momentary confusion. Two with one bullet. Not possible. Only one explanation. He and another rifleman had, by the wildest of coincidences, triggered at precisely the same moment. He quickly levered another shell into the breech and darted glances ahead and left and right.

The other rider appeared from his left, emerging from a copse north of the trail, also with rifle at the ready. He waited. The rider paused a moment, rising in stirrups to stare to the flat area across which the other jack-rabbits were disappearing from view. Then he was being studied. With his left thumb, he nudged his Stetson off his brow and waited a full minute. Not till the other rider sheathed a Winchester did he sheathe his. Slowly, a smart-stepping bay carried the other shooter toward him.

'Ranch-hand, and young,' was his first guess.

The rider's rig suggested this. Batwing chaps over Levis, a cotton shirt under a denim jacket, polka-dot bandanna knotted at the neck, Stetson with a chin-cord aslant on the dark head. Then he was hailed by name and his eyebrows shot up.

'Larry Valentine. That's who you are, and don't tell me I'm mistaken.'

The voice was undeniably female. A woman with hair cut so short was a rarity in the 1880s – but rigged in male garb? He rallied from his shock and lifted his hat to her.

'Sonofagun,' he breathed.

She chuckled good-humouredly, brown eyes sparkling, white teeth flashing. One damn good-looking woman, he observed. Hers was the pleasing face of a – how old could she be? He figured twenty-five at most.

'If you could see the look on your face,' she teased. Then she stopped smiling. 'If you could've seen the look on *my* face when I saw two rabbits go down. What would you say – one chance in a thousand? Two shots, but I only heard one.'

'Me too,' he nodded, staring past her toward the copse. 'Got friends waitin' for you back there?' She shook her head. 'You're travellin' alone?'

'I can see you disapprove,' she said. 'Well, that tallies with all I've heard and read of you and your partner. It offends your southern chivalry, meeting a woman travelling alone and dressed as a man.'

'I guess you got your reasons, ma'am,' he said.

Her face clouded over. She averted her gaze for a moment.

'Yes, good reasons – to put it mildly. I had no option but to make this search by myself, but don't assume I didn't count the risks. I almost wept when I cut my hair.'

'So you could pass for a man,' he guessed. 'Well, it works. But not up close.'

'It's not ma'am, it's miss,' she said. 'But I

wouldn't have approached you had I not recognized you. I suppose others have told you?'

'We look exactly like our pictures in the newspapers,' he said resentfully.

'It's true,' she said. 'Shouldn't we collect our kill now? By noon, I'm going to be hungry. I'm a little low on supplies and that cottontail's the first game I've seen in days.' She nudged the bay closer and thrust out her hand. 'Emma Dane of the Rocking D ranch, Harper County. And let's not be formal, Larry. Please call me Emma.' Her handshake was like a man's, firm, strong, warm. As they idled their mounts toward their kill, he voiced a resolve.

'I'm plenty curious, but why you're travellin' alone is nobody's business but yours, so I ain't about to pry.'

'I'm curious too,' she said. 'I've always supposed, if ever I met the famous Larry Valentine, I'd also meet his partner. You and Stretch are a matched pair, it's always said.'

'There's a reason,' he said.

'I'm sure there is,' she said. 'If you want to keep it to yourself, fine. I won't pester you with questions, but I warn you, Larry, I don't intend keeping my trouble a secret from you. Of all the men I'm apt to encounter, you're the only one I'd want to confide in – like it or not. I need to talk about it anyway.' Her next words were voiced so vehemently that he eyed her sidelong. 'It's all been locked inside of me for too long.'

'Pick your own time,' he shrugged.

They collected two plump jack-rabbits, both drilled through the head. Emma Dane was no slouch with a rifle, he reflected, as he slung the carcasses onto the pack-horse. As they rode on, he noted the Colt holstered at her right side, and she anticipated his question.

'Yes, I'm just as accurate with a handgun. It comes of being born and raised on a ranch.'

'But not educated in no cowtown schoolhouse,' he opined.

'No,' she said. 'Rocking D was raising prime beef. My parents – may they rest in peace – sent me to a good school in Carson City. My brother ...' her face clouded over again, 'my young, headstrong and foolish brother, had the same opportunity but refused it.' She brooded a moment before putting a question to him; the way she voiced it, he couldn't take offence. 'I hope you and Stretch are never self-conscious about having so little schooling? You shouldn't be. After all, you both had honourable intentions when you ran away. The war had just begun. You were mere boys, but with a sense of duty, so you just had to enlist.'

'It don't bother us none,' he assured her. 'Sometimes, when high-educated folks talk fancy, we don't savvy what they're sayin', but that don't matter. Most folks savvy what *we're* sayin'.'

She leaned forward in her saddle, studying the surface of the trail.

'Horse-tracks,' she observed. 'You're following them?' He nodded. 'How many horses?'

'Seven,' he said.

'Are you certain?' she asked. Then she shook her head impatiently. 'I should beg your pardon. Of course you're certain. You and Stretch, expert at reading sign. Too bad.'

'Too bad?' he prodded.

'I'm seeking track of only six riders,' she explained. 'That's how many of them there are, the Pronto Gang.'

'The what?'

'You've not heard of those outlaws?'

'It's a while since we last saw Nevada.'

'Six of them.' In her precise way, Emma Dane related the known information on the wolf-pack still eluding state and Federal lawmen. 'They could be on record, but nobody can be sure because they're never seen without their masks. I don't mean bandannas.'

'Hoods,' guessed Larry.

'And you've probably guessed how they earned their name,' she continued. 'They strike suddenly. Whether robbing a bank or holding up a stage, they just seem to arrive without warning, they're suddenly there. It's also known they're based somewhere in the high country east, the Sierra Solitario, lawmen believe. But no posse has solved the riddle of just where that hideout is, so it must be heavily camouflaged.' She was silent a long moment. Eyeing her covertly, admiring her face in profile, he forced himself to patience. Whatever confidence this resolute woman meant to share with him, she would take her time about it. 'An impossible task – but I have to try.'

They rode another forty yards, he warily scanning the terrain ahead.

'Try what?' he asked.

'I have to find that robbers' roost,' she said firmly. 'I have no choice, Larry, because I believe my brother is with them. Voluntarily, not as a prisoner.'

He studied her again.

'It cost you somethin' to tell me that,' he frowned. 'The words didn't come easy.'

'Don't worry,' she said. 'I'm not about to lose control, break down and weep. I've steeled myself to live with my problem – and my grief.'

'What're we talkin' about here?' he challenged. 'You think you can find a hideaway no search-party ever even got close to, talk horse sense to your kid brother and take him away from an owlhoot bunch ...?'

'I know it seems an impossible task – I already said that, didn't I?' she retorted. 'I also said I have no choice. Do you imagine this is my idea of fun, for pity's sake? Damn it, Larry, I don't even have a plan. I have to take it one step at a time. First I must find the hideout. After that, I'll just have to plot my next move, work out some kind of strategy. I hope none of this is irritating you. I did warn you I intend confiding in you, and that means everything.'

'Uh-huh,' he grunted. 'Like it or not, you said.'

'We've known each other little more than an hour and already I'm getting on your nerves,' she said contritely.

'No,' he said. 'I'm plenty patient with folks that's got trouble, but *you're* gonna have to be patient, Emma.' He indicated the tracks they were following. 'Seven horses I said. If you think your kid brother's the seventh rider, forget it. Sorry. It couldn't be the kid.'

'Well, of course it couldn't be,' she shrugged. 'These tracks are too fresh. I was delayed. A lot of time has passed since he disappeared, and Harper County's many a long day's ride from here.' She gestured. 'Far to the north.'

'All right now, time enough later for us to parley,' he said. 'We're headed into open country and I'll be takin' us into all the cover I can find. I figure the hombres I've been bird-doggin' got to be a day and a half ahead, but that's no guarantee one of 'em ain't fallin' back to check the ground they've travelled.'

'We can't afford to be seen,' she agreed.

'So no more palaver till we're nooncamped and eatin',' he cautioned. 'I can't hunt cover and listen to talk at the same time. No matter what you've heard about Stretch and me, we ain't perfect. Only human, you know? Else we'd never have rid into an ambush and, believe me, we've rid into plenty.'

A little before noon, he chose a temporary campsite, the near base of a towering, massive rock-mound north of the trail. Emma Dane at once offered to gather firewood and was told nothing doing. She could skin and gut their lunch. He would choose the wood for their cookfire, the faint smoke of which would not be visible from the north.

'Short on coffee, huh?' he surmised, when he had seen to the three horses and had a fire going.

'I have enough left for a couple of cups apiece.'

'Fine. We'll use what's left of yours. Plenty more on the pack-critter. I got corn bread too. We might's well eat it with this meat. By sundown, it won't taste so good. Stale and hard, you know?'

Over the flames, while the coffee-pot chattered, they roasted chunks of jack-rabbit. She was hungry. This was obvious enough, the way she concentrated on eating her share. Probably she had skipped breakfast, he supposed. She accounted for wedges of corn bread just as hungrily.

Not until they were sipping coffee did she begin talking again, this time in greater detail, taking him completely into her confidence. He didn't need this. Too bad about her trouble. He was sympathetic but, hell's sakes, he had his own problem, a big one.

As her story unfolded, he watched her face, reading her changing expressions. He sought no involvement with the opposite sex, never had, never would. Incurable wanderlust and matrimony are a bad mix. For the first time in a long time, however, he admitted to himself that, were he the kind who could settle down, take a woman as his wife and stay loyal to her the rest of his life, it would have to be a woman like Emma Dane.

THREE

Blueprint for Tragedy

'I've been running Rocking D since the death of my father two years ago,' she began.

'Good guess,' he congratulated himself.

'You mean ...?' she frowned.

'No offence.' He showed her a wry grin. 'Somethin' about you. I had you pegged for a woman of the kind that takes charge, a natural boss.' He took another mouthful of coffee. 'Go on. Tell it all.'

'My mother died many years before,' she continued. 'That would've been three years after she gave birth to my brother Clifford, called Cliff. He'd be nineteen now – just.'

'Not much younger'n his sister,' he suggested.

'Trying to cheer me up?' She smiled, but briefly. 'I'm twenty-five and, since Dad died, I've tried to be parent as well as big sister. Nice compliment, Larry. I don't delude myself. I know I could pass for thirty.'

'No, you couldn't either,' he said. 'But keep talkin'.'

'I already called Cliff foolish and headstrong, and that's no lie,' she said bitterly. 'He became worse after Dad's death. Life on a working ranch – we're running three thousand head, so Rocking D is no two-bit concern – was never his idea of a good time. He resented all the chores, though he's healthy and strong, good with horses and cattle, as expert as any hand on our payroll. Not enough excitement for him. He wanted more. And he tends to be disrespectful of lawmen.'

Was this disrespect justified? No. The sheriff of Harper County, which covered a lot of territory, was a dedicated, incorruptible and never lazy lawman, as were his deputies. There were, in the county seat, several worthy citizens who would have aided Emma in curbing her unruly brother, perhaps influencing him to tread the straight and narrow. The sheriff, a local doctor, the schoolmaster and the mayor, all close friends of the late Clem and Sophie Dane. But Rocking D was better than a day's ride from the county seat, situated less than a hundred yards from the county's east border, so visits to town were few and far between. Rocking D was as much a small community as a cattle spread; four of the hired hands were married and raising children, living in good cabins set apart from the bunkhouse.

'A good place to live,' Emma said wistfully. 'I love it there. Cliff just didn't. He had ambition, but the wrong kind, Larry. I give thanks my father didn't live to hear of his son's stupid ambition. Outlaws are his heroes.'

'Damn fool kid,' scowled Larry.

'He thinks of them as the real adventurers of the West, men to be admired,' she went on. 'Most of all, he admired the Pronto Gang. So smart, he used to enthuse, always one jump ahead of the law. And he yearned to be one of them.'

'Better you should've kept him hogtied,'

muttered Larry.

'I kept a wary eye on him as much as was possible,' she assured him. 'But, some time ago, there were two disasters, both on the same day – and that's how I lost Cliff. You and Stretch grew up in cattle country, so what can I tell you about a stampede that you don't already know?'

'Bad medicine.'

'Yes. As much a calamity as anthrax to ranch folk. I don't know how it started – that's often the way, isn't it? Well, the whole herd stampeded northward, and you know the routine. Every man able to sit a saddle rides out to head them off.'

'You too?'

'Of course.'

'Yeah. Of course.'

'I lost sight of Cliff and, while Rocking D was having trouble, there was more of it in the county seat. The Pronto Gang held up a bank, looted the safe, mortally wounded a cashier and, on their way out of town, did so much shooting that everybody, including the county law officers, had to scatter for cover. But Sheriff Reardon eventually organized a posse, better than a dozen angry townsmen, and pursued the robbers south. Maybe they'd have overtaken them …'

'Or ridden into an ambush,' said Larry.

'We'll never know,' Emma said grimly. 'Because the posse had to turn back from Legget's Gorge. The timber bridge was afire by the time they reached the north edge, and they had no doubt the fugitives started it burning after they crossed over. That would've been easy enough. The bridge was old. Planks mostly. And ample dry brush along the south edge.'

'Maybe that posse got off light,' said Larry. 'Most bandidos're kill-crazy anyway. Six of 'em?'

'All wearing hoods.'

'Some turkey-shoot it could've been, if they'd spread 'emselves along the south side, waited for the posse to get halfway across and opened up on 'em with rifles.'

'That didn't happen, fortunately,' murmured Emma. 'And Cliff hasn't been seen since, so I believe *my* theory is correct. The outlaws didn't set that bridge afire. My brother did.'

Larry drained his cup, grimaced and fished out his makings.

'You think he ...?'

'If he was in that area, if he saw six hooded riders cross the bridge, he'd jump to the obvious conclusion,' she declared. 'Too great a temptation, Larry. He assumed they'd been pursued from the county seat. Here was his big chance to win favour with the kind of rogues he so admired. So he crossed the bridge and *he* collected brush, dumped it on those old planks and set it afire. Don't tell me that's a wild guess. I *know* him. And I believe he then caught up with the bank-robbers, bragged of stalling the posse and invited himself to join them. It would've taken Sheriff Reardon's party a whole day or more to reach the south side, a steep descent of the north wall, then a long climb to reach the south edge.'

He drew a twig from the dying fire, got his cigarette working and eyed her thoughtfully.

'All right, if that's what you believe, *I* got to believe it. So who else knows?'

'Not a soul but me – until now,' she said softly. 'And I wouldn't have told you, knowing how you despise outlaws, if I weren't sure I could trust you.'

'I ain't about to blab to the first tin star I see – not that we're apt to find a town hereabouts – but you'd better believe this,' he growled. 'If I ever caught up with your kid brother, I'd kick his butt so hard ...'

'After *I'm* through with him.' Her growl was as ferocious as his, much to his approval; little danger he and Emma would quarrel, certainly not about the actions of her wayward brother. 'Meanwhile, I can only pray he's alive and well – and maybe having second thoughts. I lost so much time, Larry. It's taken me till today to find a trail leading to the Sierra Solitario.'

'Took more'n a day to head off them stampeders and round up the strays,' he supposed.

'Longer than that,' she complained. 'And there was a further delay. My foreman, Dad's old friend Tim Gallaher, went down with some kind of fever the day we got back to the ranch.'

'Had to be *you* doctored him?' he frowned.

'I'm the ranch-boss,' she said. 'I have to take on all manner of chores. Why, I even delivered the first-born of two of the hired hands. I couldn't leave Uncle Tim in somebody else's care.'

'So you couldn't get away till after the fever broke,' he nodded.

'All anybody at Rocking D knows is that I'm looking for Cliff,' she said. 'Uncle Tim's back on his feet now. He can run the place for – as long as it takes me to do what I have to do.' Her next move caught him off-guard and started his pulse pounding. Impulsively, she reached for his free hand, grasping it in both of hers. 'Larry, I thought

I had the courage to go it alone. But, now that we've met – must I beg? Please, Larry! You're so experienced. You have to help me!'

'*Don't* beg.' His retort was just as impulsive. 'Not from me. And – uh – I'm gonna need that hand sometime.'

'I'm sorry,' she said, letting go. 'I'm not always so emotional. I guess – it's time I admitted to myself – I'm getting desperate. Not just desperate. Frantic.'

'Sure,' he said. 'But, travellin' together, we won't help kid brother or ourselves 'less we hang onto our nerve, both of us.'

'Then – you will?'

'Plain truth is I'd have to anyway.'

'What – does *that* mean?'

'Means I think my partner's bein' taken to the same place your brother's at.' Abruptly, Larry got to his feet. 'Somebody once said it's a small world. I guess they were right.'

'I don't understand,' said Emma.

'How in tarnation could you?' he shrugged. 'How much've I told you? Damn little. Best we keep movin'. I'll deal you in on my trouble when we get back to followin' tracks. All you need to know for starters is we're both losers. You've lost your brother. I've lost my partner.'

On the trail again, she insisted on taking a turn at leading the pack-animal.

'I don't wonder you and your friend are confirmed bachelors,' she said regretfully. 'Some women can be so selfish. All the time I've been wishing my trouble on you, you've had your own problem, your own fears. You've been more patient than I deserve.'

'One thing I've learned about females.' He threw her a sidelong grin. 'If they got their mind set on talkin', it's best to let 'em – till they're all talked out.'

'You listened to me,' she said. 'You've been patient and sympathetic. Share your problem with me now. It's my turn to listen.'

'With these tracks leadin' us east, and if the Pronto Gang's holed up in high country somewheres east, I think I've seen 'em without their hoods,' he said bluntly. 'And, to ease your mind some, your kid brother wasn't one of the six buzzards that kidnapped Stretch. None of 'em were young enough to be him.'

'Lord Almighty! You let me air my woes and, all the time, Stretch has been kidnapped – by the Pronto Gang?'

'Has to be them. All adds up, Emma. When I find my partner, I find your brother.'

'Where did it happen – and how?'

'Only way it *could* happen. We got separated.'

They were making another ascent, the trail taking them into desolate country, a wilderness of mounds and ridges and brush-clumps. He recounted the Kingsville incident in his own terse way, but comprehensively, recalling as best he could the silent and watchful half-dozen present during the late night poker party.

When he had finished, she assured him, 'You'd have had fairer treatment from Sheriff Reardon. He seeks both sides of every accusation. He'd have gone looking for witnesses to support you.'

'Well,' said Larry. 'I think Doc Bolger burned the Kingsville sheriff's ears. Appleby couldn't wait to turn me loose. Trouble is, by then, Stretch was long gone – and the buzzards that grabbed him.'

'But why would they ...?' she began. Then she winced. 'I'm sorry. That was clumsy of me. I guess their motive is clear enough. All the outlaw scum you and Stretch have accounted for, so many of them must've had ...'

'Right,' he nodded. 'Kin or friends. Others of their kind. So they're plannin' somethin' for the beanpole, and the hell of it is I can't hustle this. When I catch up with 'em, it'll have to be a surprise. If I tip my hand and they catch just a glimpse of me, they're apt to put a bullet in his head or use him as a shield.'

'This is terrible,' she fretted.

'It ain't good,' he said.

At this time, far ahead, the taller Texan was assessing his chances of escape. Too much to hope for, hands tied to his saddlehorn, feet roped to stirrups? Why the hell not? Had to do something, didn't he? They were climbing, he flanked by Stark and Ivers, Cross and Aberlain bringing up the rear, Werris and Murquette leading, Murquette holding the pinto's rein. To his left, just beyond Ivers, the trail gave way to a brushy slant, maybe not too steep for his mount to descend – if he could distract his captors just long enough.

Murquette first, he decided. Then buffet Ivers some way, get past him. These bastards wanted him alive; he was to live to suffer at the hands of their leader, so there'd be no shooting. Well, it was worth trying. Anything was better than passive submission.

Though his feet were roped, he could still use his bootheels, and did. The pinto responded quickly, surging forward, its left shoulder ramming the rump of Murquette's mount, startling it. The animal was suddenly giving Murquette trouble and, to bring it under control, Murquette released the pinto's rein. Stretch promptly keeled to his left with his head bowed. Ivers instinctively reached for him and, hard and fast, he jerked his head up, catching Iver's chin. Then he was kneeing the pinto, urging it past Ivers' animal to reach the edge of the trail, but cursing men were balking him. Cross came up fast behind him, swinging a fist.

Stretch took that blow and several others, hard blows that filled him with pain but, stubbornly, he denied his captors the satisfaction of a cry, a gasp, a grunt of protest. Cross, swearing obscenely, drew and raised his Colt, was about to swing the weapon at Stretch's head, when Werris restrained him.

'*No*, Farley!'

'Sonofabitch!' raged Cross.

'Gunwhip him and you could bust his skull!' warned Werris. 'He could die – and then you'd have Jethro to answer to.'

'And you know what that means,' muttered Stark.

Cross grimaced and holstered his pistol.

'Damn trouble-shooters – they never quit,' he scowled. 'Big heroes.'

'We'll keep goin',' said Werris. 'Carl, change places with me.'

Murquette retrieved the pinto's rein. Ivers urged his mount forward, while Werris fell back to ride at Stretch's left side. The climb was resumed and, scathingly, Werris derided him for a fool move that could never have succeeded.

'You don't have the brains you were born with, Emerson. How far did you think you could run – and what'd it get you?'

Stretch turned to match stares with him. He bled from three facial injuries, from nose, from puffy mouth. Still he managed a retort.

'Can't blame a man for tryin'.'

'It's no use tryin',' jibed Werris. 'Haven't you started *believin'* it yet? You're done for. All the showin' off, all the buttin' into every jasper's business, coverin' yourself in glory, newspapers praisin' you – it's all over. Tragg's roost's the end of the line for you. You're never gonna escape, so you'll cash in any way Tragg decides. Listen, you could get lucky. Minute he lays eyes on you, he could go trigger-happy, empty a gun into you. That way, it'll be quick.'

'Too bad you didn't fetch my irons along,' mumbled Stretch. 'You never can tell, bandido. Your boss might hanker to down me in a fair fight, might order you to give me my irons. That way, he'd have somethin' to brag about.'

'If you're crazy enough to hope for that kind of chance ...' began Werris.

'On the other hand, I might put one right 'tween Tragg's eyes,' said Stretch. 'Then I'd be one against the rest of you and it's for sure I'd get backshot, but it'd be worth dyin' for – and the Pronto Gang'd need a new boss.'

'Big talk,' jeered Werris.

'Just thinkin' out loud, Werris,' shrugged Stretch. 'Just thinkin' out loud.'

'Rough and ready and plenty tough – that's what you think you are?' challenged Werris. 'I can't wait to see how you're gonna change, hot-shot. You won't feel so tough when Jethro Tragg looks you over, when he starts figurin' his own way of squarin' accounts.'

'Vengeance,' sneered Stretch. 'For his bandido brother that was no more of a man than he is.'

Werris gasped an oath and struck at him with a fist, bloodying his left ear. That started his head aching again, but he clenched his teeth and bore with it. He put his pain-wracked eyes on Werris, and Werris couldn't meet his gaze.

'You're gettin' littler every minute, Werris,' he declared. 'No matter how tall you stand, you're little in mind and belly. When a man shoots an unarmed man or beats up on a man that can't hit back, he's lower'n a snake's belly.' He was helpless, but his next words caused Werris's scalp to crawl. 'I'll be rememberin' you, little man.'

An hour later, Larry and Emma heard the echo of a single rifle-shot far ahead. They were now following the trail through thick-timbered terrain, climbing yet another slant.

'Far off,' Larry quietly commented.

'What do you suppose ...?' began Emma.

'One of 'em, I guess,' he said. 'Might be they got many a mile to travel to the hideout. Meanwhile, they got to eat.'

'One of them shot a deer?'

'That's my hunch.'

'You've been very quiet,' she said. 'The wind's still blowing from the east, so it's safe for us to talk.'

'Sure,' he nodded. 'You got somethin' to say, go right ahead.'

'It has to be said,' she declared. 'We have to be in agreement, Larry.'

'About what?' he asked.

'You know exactly what I mean,' she chided. 'We've avoided the subject, but I believe we should clear the air and get it all out in the open. This isn't your way, Larry, and you must be hating it. The Lone Star Trouble-Shooters don't pursue outlaws with a woman tagging along.'

'Scarce ever happens,' he agreed.

'But we can't disregard the fact that we have the same goal, a shared purpose,' she pointed out. 'I have as much right as you to seek the Pronto Gang.'

'No argument,' he shrugged. 'They got your willin' brother and my unwillin' partner.'

'So we must work together, mustn't we?' she pleaded.

'You got one thing right,' he said. 'It ain't my way. But this is a special situation and, come to that, you're a special kind of woman. Any other female I'd have shook off by now, made her head back to where she came from and leave everything to me.'

She eyed him suspiciously.

'You're flattering me – but for your own reasons.'

'Tellin' it the way it is,' he countered. 'If I feared you ain't got the nerve for what's ahead of us, I'd up and say it, bet your purty hide on that.'

'You give me credit for courage,' she frowned. 'Does that mean I'm your partner, at least till it's all over? You won't order me to go hide – if there has to be fighting?'

'Don't try to coax no promises from me, Emma,' he warned. 'You know it's too early for that. When the time comes, I hope you'll stay as smart as I figure you are, smart enough to do like I tell you. It won't be me tryin' to prove I'm boss. It'll be because I have to decide what's our best chance, not just yours and mine, but your brother's and my partner's.'

She pondered that blunt statement a while. Then, 'So be it,' she nodded. 'You're the strategist. I accept that.'

After another steep ascent, he demanded more information about the rebellious Cliff Dane.

'Any chance he'll feel different about things? Is the boy all bad, foolish all the time?'

'He has his good points,' she said wistfully. 'No foul language when I'm close enough to hear. I taught him *some* manners and I know for sure he's never taken liberties with the daughters of neighbouring ranchers. Only once have I seen him drunk. After that one time, he made his own decision about liquor. He was so eager to be a real man and one of his ideas of a mark of true manhood is a man who can hold his whiskey. So he still drinks, but no more than he can handle.' She winced and shook her head. 'But there were always the other characteristics, his craving for excitement and the *hours* he spent practising with his six-gun, striving for a faster draw and greater accuracy.'

'Maybe there's hope for him,' mused Larry. 'He's had time, right? Time enough to size up the bunch he's with now, study on 'em?'

'I suppose,' she said.

'Outlaws were his heroes, you told me,' he said. 'Well, now that he's one of 'em, maybe he'll wise up.'

'See them for what they are?'

'Sure. For what they *really* are. Right now, he could be wishin' he'd never quit home.'

'I can but hope,' said Emma.

The ascent was easier on the horses now, not so steep. They were approaching a curve of the trail. Whatever was beyond was anybody's guess, so Larry eased the pace, held his rein left-handed and let right hand hang close to holster. Emma followed his example.

And then the gut-chilling sounds reached them.

'Indians!' she breathed.

'Only one,' growled Larry.

Yes, only one of the voices was human, and the whooping was shriller than the whoops of white ranch-hands rounding up cattle. The whooper was undoubtedly redskin and in fear for his life, because the other voice was animal and threatening, a ferocious snarling that quickened Emma's pulse.

'Cougar!' she gasped, making to unsheathe her rifle.

Larry was several jumps ahead of her, hustling his sorrel to the bend, his Winchester out and cocked. She rounded the curve seconds behind him and the scene she now beheld was to stay in her memory the rest of her days.

A rope had been secured to a tree-limb jutting over the trail. From its other end, his moccasined feet some twenty-four inches from the ground, dangled the pudgy redman, the noose tight under his armpits, his feet free but his hands tied behind him. His face bled. So did the gash along the rump of the mountain lion poised atop a high boulder ten feet from the live, helpless bait. Maybe the beast would leap at the redman. Maybe it would drop from the rock to claw the wildly kicking legs. Either way, the beast's prey would have had no chance of survival.

Larry was rising in his stirrups, taking aim at the moment the big cat gathered itself to leap. His target was its head and, when he fired, he scored. No more pain for the beast; from atop the rock, it slid to the ground, flopping in a lifeless heap. The hanging redman heaved a sigh of relief, still swaying, his dark eyes focusing on his rescuer.

'Lawrence – dear cohort!' he cried. 'I praise and thank the Great Spirit! You – of all people – at the eleventh hour – with the prospect of my suffering an agonizing death …!'

'He – *couldn't* be an Indian!' exclaimed Emma.

Plainly, she was doubting the evidence of her ears, unable to match the flabby redman's appearance to his mode of speech.

'You got an explanation comin', but it'll have to wait,' said Larry, dismounting. 'Chief, I ain't cuttin' you free. No tellin' how useful some extra rope'll be. You just – uh – keep on a'danglin', give me time to loose them knots.'

He clambered up the tree trunk and along the branch to straddle it and work on the rope. To give him slack, Emma swung down, took the sorrel's rein and led it forward to enable the redman to straddle it. With the line no longer taut, Larry could more easily untie the knots.

The line snaked down. The cougar's almost-victim slid from Larry's saddle while he climbed down and, after a moment of hesitation, Emma began working on the rope securing his wrists.

'Hold still,' she ordered.

But he twisted to gawk at her and dazedly

observe, 'One shock after another – is there to be no limit? You are unquestionably female, good lady, but in male attire and – ye gods – short-haired!'

'I don't believe *any* of this,' she complained to Larry. 'He *is* an Indian but – I must be cracking – his diction, his command of English – just isn't *possible*!'

'You'll have to stay curious a while,' said Larry, as the pudgy one surveyed him in relief and abject gratitude. 'Talk to me, Chief. Did six white polecats do this to you?'

'Woodville is with them,' mumbled Cathcart P. Slow Wolf. Emma untied the last knot. His hands free, he gripped Larry's shoulders. 'He is their prisoner, Lawrence. Despite my terror, I pretended not to recognize him. And – he had the wisdom to do likewise.' He gestured eastward. 'They ...'

'I know they're headed east and I know they got Stretch,' nodded Larry. 'They take your horse?'

'I left it tied ...' This time, the portly half-Sioux gestured northward. 'I deemed it wiser to stalk the wounded cougar afoot, but then I ...'

'All right now, we're gonna have to powwow, but first you better fetch your horse,' urged Larry.

'Must confess I fear for the unfortunate animal,' Slow Wolf mumbled. 'So much confusion. Could the cougar have slain it before those blackguards seized me ...?'

'Only one way to find out,' said Larry.

He bent to pick up a battered beaver hat from the band of which a turkey feather jutted. The redman thanked him, donned his headgear, then thought to doff it to bug-eyed Emma.

'Delighted to meet you, dear lady. Would that the circumstances were more conducive to the social pleasantries.'

'I think I'm losing my mind,' fretted Emma, slumping against Larry.

'Would you relieve me of an embarrassment?' Slow Wolf begged. 'She's entitled to an explanation – the truth about me.'

'Sure you want me to tell her?' asked Larry.

'It always distresses me,' said Slow Wolf. 'Must I repeat myself, deliver another discourse on the disadvantages of my racial origins? Coming from you, my good friend, it will be more succinct, easier for her to comprehend.'

'He speaks better English than *you* do!' she gasped.

'Most everybody does,' shrugged Larry, as they watched Slow Wolf pad into the thick brush north of the bend. 'Better get the load off. We got nothin' to do but wait, and there's no guessing how soon he'll be back.' Emma sank to the ground, tugged off her Stetson and shook her head wearily. He hunkered beside her and began building a smoke. 'First thing you'd better savvy about that half-Injun is he's an old buddy of Stretch and me. We trust him. He trusts us. So you can trust him. No matter how he looks to you, he's a genuine, regular gentleman.'

'A half-breed?' she frowned.

'Half-Sioux,' he nodded. 'His pa was a full-blood. His momma was as white as you or me.'

'But – he looks ...'

'Yep. Looks all Injun. Got his pa's looks and his pa's Injun savvy, but Mrs Slow Wolf was a schoolmarm and, from her, he learned his English

– high-class English.'

'This is incredible, Larry. It's – all so bizarre that – if I hadn't heard what he said and the way he said it, the way he expresses himself, I couldn't believe it possible. How *can* it be possible? You say he's half-Sioux. So a white woman, a schoolteacher and therefore a lady of education – mating with a full-blood redskin?'

'Crazy kind of story, kind of comical too.' Though deeply concerned for the survival of his partner, Larry was grinning. Any recollection of the circumstances of Slow Wolf's birth tended to nudge the funny bone. 'If you want to hear it …'

'I *have* to hear it,' Emma declared. 'My curiosity is killing me, so have mercy. Make me understand.'

'It ain't all that mysterious,' he assured her. 'When I've told it all, it'll make sense, you'll see.'

FOUR

The Hoolahan Expedition

Biographical background on Cathcart P. Slow Wolf had a strong element of humour; Emma was suppressing giggles long before the story ended.

It began better than twenty-seven years before when an impulsive and not too bright brave of the Boysen Mesa tribe, whose chief at that time was Black Horse, rabble-roused other braves into daubing themselves with war paint, after which he led a spectacularly unsuccessful raid on a wagon-train. The not too bright brave was Slow Wolf senior.

Because the raiders telegraphed their intentions with war whoops, the hardy pioneers had ample time for forming their Conestoga wagons into a circle and improvising barricades from behind which they proceeded to give their attackers an extremely hard time. The raid was doomed to failure, Slow Wolf understandably disgruntled at this reflection on his leadership qualities. Determined to seize loot of some kind – any kind – he charged a barricade, leapt his pony over it, intercepted a running woman and lifted her to his mount – and kept going.

His captive, all he had to show for this unauthorized raid, was Miss Cornelia Cathcart, a schoolteacher neither young nor beautiful. So heavy were the casualties inflicted by the sharpshooters of the wagon-train that Black Horse and his underchiefs denounced Slow Wolf as a bungling buck, a muddle-headed misfit and a stupid Sioux. Women being so unpredictable, Miss Cathcart sprang to Slow Wolf's defence, subjecting the chief and every other Sioux of Boysen Mesa to a long-winded reprimand, a veritable torrent of abuse which inspired Black Horse to punish Slow Wolf in what seemed the most suitable way.

No. Neither Slow Wolf nor Miss Cathcart burned at the stake, though Black Horse's medicine-man strongly recommended this. At the chief's insistence, they were married in a Sioux ceremony, then banished from the tribe.

After this humiliating expulsion, the mismatched pair found their way to the settlement of Gorth, Nebraska, where Cornelia arranged what she termed a more formal marriage, this time Baptist. A schoolteacher was desperately needed in Gorth, so the locals did not balk at appointing the white wife of an exiled Sioux to that position.

And so, while Slow Wolf made his living as a hunter and trapper, his spouse tutored the small fry of Gorth. Slow Wolf junior first saw the light of day some ten and a half months later. As a child, he learned to read sign and hunt game, absorbing all the Sioux savvy of his grumpy sire, and was also taught his three 'R's by his mother. The English language was Cornelia's specialty and her son her most receptive pupil.

'By the time his folks died, he was full-grown and there was nothin' for him in his old hometown,' Larry explained in conclusion. 'He couldn't go back to his pa's people, even though he looked like a full-blood, so he just struck out on his own.'

'And you and Stretch eventually met him,' guessed Emma.

'In a Wyomin' jail,' said Larry. 'Town called Colfax. Our trails've crossed many a time since. He's saved our hides and we've saved his.'

'So there's a bond,' she said. 'Mutual trust?'

'Right,' he nodded. 'But you have to understand why only them that get close to him know he's so high-educated. He has to keep it a secret and pretend he's just a dumb Injun. You know how some folks are, a lot of whites that can scarce read nor write. They hear an Injun palaverin' fine English, it kind of irks 'em, they're apt to turn mean.'

'Yes,' she frowned. 'It can be a disadvantage, even dangerous for him.'

'So now you've heard it all,' he shrugged. 'And, when he gets back to us, it'll be his turn to do some explainin'.'

'What does the P stand for?' she asked.

'Pettigrew,' said Larry. 'His full handle's Cathcart Pettigrew Slow Wolf, but he's mostly called Slow Wolf. Stretch and me call him Chief.'

Slow Wolf rejoined them a few minutes later, leading a saddled dun with a packroll and empty rifle-scabbard secured. He was anxious about Stretch, to whom he always referred by his given name, and curious about Emma, but Larry insisted, 'You first. Tell us how come you tangled with the skunks we're tailin', then I'll explain about Emma and me.'

'By misfortune, I happened to be hunting deer in this region,' sighed the flabby one, as Larry built a cigarette for him. He accepted the quirley and a light, puffed gratefully and continued. 'I heard a rifle-shot and the cry of a cougar in pain. It was obvious to me the beast had been wounded, not slain – and you know what *that* means."

'When a hunter only wounds a big cat ...' began Larry.

'It's his responsibility to find it and finish it off,' nodded Emma. 'An unwritten but vital law. A mountain lion slowed down by a wound can't stalk smaller animals, so no human is safe.'

'There was no second shot, so I had to assume the hunter had done the unforgivable,' said Slow Wolf. He matched stares with the intrigued Emma. 'As Lawrence has – I hope – informed you, I am a hermit and a dedicated coward, but I do have my standards. I felt compelled to seek the wounded beast and put it out of its misery.'

'You didn't find the cat, but you found the scum that took Stretch prisoner,' guessed Larry.

'Clumsily stumbled onto this trail,' mumbled Slow Wolf. He winced, plagued by terrifying memories. 'Of course they had to amuse themselves. Could such rogues resist the impulse to inflict bodily harm on a redskin? Naturally they also stole my rifle.' His gaze switched to Larry. 'A fine Winchester, your gift to me, old friend.'

'And then they ...?' prodded Emma.

'I feared they would shoot me or perhaps slash my throat,' he muttered. 'But they had a more fiendish notion. I was bleeding from a facial wound. They counted on the beast they'd wounded catching the scent of my blood, so they – well – you saw how they left me.'

'Live bait for a pain-crazy mountain cat,' Larry said in disgust. He couldn't hold back from glaring at Emma. 'Fine bunch your brother threw in with.'

'How do you suppose I feel?' she retorted.

'All right, Chief, I'm gonna tell you where we're headed and why,' said Larry. 'And it'd be kind of handy havin' you along with us. You'll have a Winchester for protection when the time comes.' He jerked a thumb, indicating the pack-horse. 'They grabbed the beanpole, but left his hardware behind.' In terse sentences and with Slow Wolf listening intently, he recounted the circumstances of his partner's disappearance, repeated all Emma had told him of the Pronto Gang and, with her permission, confided her reason for running the desperadoes to ground. 'That's all of it. We don't know how big a mess the kid's got himself into. Maybe he's ridden with a raidin' party, maybe not.'

'Dear lady.' Slow Wolf waxed solicitous. 'How distraught you must be. I'm profoundly sorry.'

'Thank you,' she said. 'There's a first time for everything, Chief. I've never anticipated inviting an Indian to call me by my given name, but this just doesn't seem the time for standing on ceremony. I'm Emma Dane. It's nice to be called dear lady, but you might as well make it Emma.'

'Stretch looked bad, huh?' prodded Larry.

'He travels astride, but as their prisoner,' sighed Slow Wolf. 'Hands tied to the pinto's pommel, feet lashed to the stirrups. I believe he's been struck several times, but take heart, Lawrence. At least he's alive.' After a moment of hesitation, he decided, 'I will join you in your quest. I'm terrified of course. One encounter with those sadists was more than enough – downright nightmarish – but I feel committed. You have saved my worthless life, my friend, and not for the first time.'

'So now we go on,' said Emma.

'Time to get movin' again,' nodded Larry. 'And, as if you ain't noticed, it's gettin' colder the higher we travel. Chief, you know what we'll need by sundown, a place to nightcamp, a fire that won't give our position away, so keep your eyes peeled.'

While the bandit-hunters quit the scene of the pudgy half-breed's ordeal, five Pinkerton detectives rode into Alvarado, seat of Diego County, a mining centre sixty miles south of the Sierra Solitario. In command, and making sure everybody knew it, was a senior investigator of the famous agency, Daniel Patrick Hoolahan by name.

Deputy Sheriff Eric Lochner was slumped in his boss's desk chair and idly reading the latest edition of the *County Messenger* when the burly, florid and bumptious Hoolahan marched into the law office. To Hoolahan's disapproval and to the amusement of two of his aides, Agents Casey and Zimmerman, the deputy did not stand to attention; he merely ran an eye over the strangers, nodded lazily and said, 'Howdy.'

'Identify yourself,' ordered Hoolahan.

'You first,' invited Lochner.

'What?' scowled Hoolahan.

'Well, I know who *I* am,' shrugged the deputy. 'You can see my star, so you know I belong here. But I never saw you gents before.'

'I am Chief Investigator Daniel P. Hoolahan of

the Pinkerton Agency and these are my aides,' Hoolahan announced threateningly.

'Take your word for it – no need to holler,' Lochner said mildly. 'Lochner's my moniker. I'm a deputy here. Call me Eric.'

'I don't deal with underlings, Deputy,' growled Hoolahan. 'My business is of the utmost urgency and included in my credentials is a document issued by the Department of Justice instructing all lawmen of this state to accord me the fullest co-operation. Right now, I'll have you know, that makes me the senior law authority of Diego County. Where is your superior?'

'You mean Jeff, the sheriff?' asked Lochner.

'Well,' sneered Hoolahan, 'I certainly don't mean the shiftless Mexican stablehand who's tending our horses.'

'Unless,' Agent Casey dared suggest, '*he* happens to be the sheriff.'

'No levity, Casey,' chided Hoolahan.

'You must've checked your critters into the B and J livery,' said Lochner. 'That's the only barn got a Mex hostler. Juan's his name. Juan Rojas.'

'The devil with stablehands!' blustered Hoolahan. 'Who is sheriff and why isn't he in his office?'

Eric Lochner was willing to answer all questions, even from a proddy Pinkerton.

'Jeff Breakstone's sheriff and the reason he ain't here is he's someplace else, meanin' Quilley's Saloon a block uptown. Oh, and if you should happen to want Chief Deputy Falk, that's where he's at too. I'm mindin' the office on account of Jeff and Zack both got thirsty at the same time.'

'Isn't this typical?' Hoolahan complained to his aides.

'Well, certainly,' nodded Agent Zimmerman. 'It's that time of afternoon, Dan. Matter of fact, I could use a little appetizer myself. What do you say, Case?'

'Sounds good to me,' said Casey.

'Confound it, do I have to remind you of the importance of our mission?' challenged Hoolahan. 'To the Pinkerton Agency has fallen a great responsibility. We are committed to the heavy task of apprehending the infamous Pronto Gang.'

He grimaced resentfully as Lochner loosed a low whistle and remarked, 'That'd be some helluva coup – if you could bring it off.'

'So – uh – next stop Quilley's Saloon,' suggested Casey.

'It seems we have no choice,' grouched Hoolahan, and he led the Pinkertons out.

Up to the next block they marched and into the saloon. The Quilley establishment was well-patronized at this time by regular pre-supper topers, two of whom were the lean, short-bearded Sheriff Jefferson Breakstone and the heavy-set Deputy Zachary Falk, easily identified by their badges.

Advanced upon while sharing a corner table, the local lawmen warily appraised the assertive Hoolahan, Falk observing, 'They look like a reasonable bunch, all but their boss.'

'Chip on his shoulder,' opined Breakstone. 'A bigmouth used to gettin' his own way.'

Reaching the corner, Hoolahan announced himself loudly; Quilley, his staff and customers could never be unaware five Pinkertons had arrived. Breakstone nodded affably and invited the detectives to pull up chairs. Hoolahan insisted he'd do his talking on his feet, while Casey, Zimmerman and the other two converged on a congenial bartender, intent on ridding their throats of trail-dust.

Presented with the boss-Pinkerton's letters of authority, the sheriff perused and returned them.

'Clear enough, Mister Hoolahan …' he began.

'Special Agent Hoolahan,' insisted Hoolahan.

'Well, okay,' shrugged Breakstone. 'I was gonna invite you to call me Jeff like most folks do, but I just changed my mind. You can call me Sheriff. As for all this co-operation I'm bound to give, all you have to do is ask – and I'll see what I can do.'

Still at top volume, and to the keen interest of all present, Hoolahan announced that a cousin of a member of the U.S. Senate had been one of the fatalities of a recent raid by the elusive Pronto Gang, the Settlers National Bank at Grant City, central Nevada. The senator had brought pressure to bear on the Department of Justice, and thanks to its formidable reputation, the Pinkerton Agency had been retained to achieve what all other law enforcement officers had failed to do – locate and apprehend the homicidal bandits.

'Senator Madigan's kinsman cut down in the main street!' boomed Hoolahan. 'An unarmed visitor to Grant City!'

'Also a deputy sheriff, it says in the newspapers,' Falk thought to point out. 'Also an old lady that couldn't move fast enough to get clear of the shootin', and a fifteen-year-old boy wounded so bad he'll be on crutches the rest of his life.'

'*No* citizen of *any* town is safe while those hooded desperadoes ride free, striking at will!'

warned Hoolahan. 'They have to be found and brought to trial, and that's why I'm here.'

'You won't find 'em here in Alvarado,' protested Quilley, the saloon-keeper.

'Now, Special Agent Hoolahan, you must've heard no searchers ever could find the gang's hideaway,' drawled Breakstone. 'It's pretty certain they're holed up somewheres in the Sierra Solitario, but nobody knows where.'

An off-duty mine-hand at the bar assured Hoolahan, 'Ain't never been a posse even got close.'

'I'm not proposing a search-party nor a mere posse!' declared Hoolahan. 'This is to be an *expedition*, by thunder! And I mean well-equipped, well-armed and with an experienced guide at my service, preferably an ex-army scout, but I won't reject an Indian, provided he's reliable. There *has* to be a trail to the gang's hideout, *has* to be a way in. That entrance has not yet been discovered but, damn it, it must exist!'

'Has to be found sooner or later, I'll grant you,' shrugged Falk.

'Sooner the better!' snapped Hoolahan. 'Great balls of fire! Do you think the Pinkerton Agency or the United States government will tolerate outrages perpetrated by the Pronto Gang, the looting, the killing, *indefinitely*? They've run roughshod over the law for far too long already, and now the time has come to organize, to venture deep and high into the Sierra Solitario, root out those butchers and bring them to justice and, by Saint Patrick, if they offer resistance, we'll massacre 'em, wipe 'em from the face of the earth!'

The locals were impressed. They drank and

listened, some of them overawed by the boss-Pinkerton's thunderous rhetoric. Casey, Zimmerman and the other two Pinkertons drank, but did not listen. They had heard it all before; one Hoolahan harangue was pretty much the same as another.

'You said "we"?' frowned Breakstone.

'You've seen the authority invested in me,' said Hoolahan. 'It's my intention to mount my expedition here in Alvarado. I of course will be the leader. You and one of your deputies will be required, also the aforementioned tracker and at least seven more men who won't balk at the prospect of a shooting-fight.' This announcement triggered a rumble of comment. He raised his hands, bellowed for silence and played his trump card. 'All volunteers accepted by me will be paid by the day – every day we're gone from Alvarado. Moreover, when the outlaws become our prisoners, there'll be a handsome bonus for everybody.'

'Who's puttin' up the dinero?' a barkeep wanted to know.

Hoolahan squared his shoulders, thrust his paunch out, reverently removed his derby and held it to his chest.

'The government of these United States!' he informed one and all. '*That's* who's paying for everything; provisions, arms and ammunition, rental of horses, your time and efforts – everything!' He turned to challenge the bemused sheriff. 'How about that guide?'

Breakstone consulted his senior deputy.

'Think Paiute Jake'd be interested?'

'Jake's good,' Falk conceded. 'As good as you'll

get.' To Hoolahan he remarked, 'You wouldn't find a smarter scout in the whole state, but that's no guarantee he'll steer us to the hideout. He can't work no miracles.'

'If he's the best, get him,' ordered Hoolahan. 'And now ...' he eyed Quilley's regulars sternly, 'I will interview volunteers. By suppertime, I have to know how many are joining us, for I don't mean to linger in Alvarado. We will start for the Sierra Solitario at first light tomorrow.'

After three adventurous locals lined up to be interviewed, five others followed suit.

'Dan'll get what he wants,' Casey predicted to his old cohort Zimmerman. 'Biggest force ever rode out of this burg.'

'Oh, sure,' agreed Zimmerman. 'Dan always gets his way. We'll have an expedition, no denying that. But the big question is will we ever end up where he wants us to be – in the Pronto Gang's home camp?'

'Yeah,' nodded Casey. 'That's the big question.'

Led by their apprehensive ally, Larry and Emma began another ascent. The shadows of late afternoon were lengthening and, thanks to the altitude, the atmosphere becoming chillier. They had donned ponchos and now, automatically, Slow Wolf had assumed the duty of tracking their quarry.

After that ascent ended, they paused to parley.

'The bunch we're tailin' have to nightcamp again,' Larry pointed out. 'So, while there's still light enough, we got to find *us* a windbreak – and wood enough to keep us from freezin' till we move again.'

'You would not attempt a rescue in daylight,' guessed Slow Wolf. 'To do so would be to put our friend Woodville's life in jeopardy. With him as their hostage ...'

'You're readin' my mind, Chief,' said Larry.

'But, under cover of darkness?' asked Slow Wolf.

'It's a chance,' frowned Larry. 'Depends on us findin' 'em before sun-up. I figure one lookout. If I can settle his hash quiet, we'll maybe get the drop on the rest of 'em before they rouse.'

'So we'll have to break camp long before dawn,' Emma said. 'Yes, that makes good sense. We take turns to sleep after a good supper, then we can move again as early as you wish.'

Their pudgy guide found a position ideal for their purpose some short distance north of the trail, a rocky overhang. Humans and animals would be shielded from the night cold and, if they were lucky, their fire would warm the rock, generating extra, much-needed heat.

Emma broke out provisions while Larry saw to the horses and Slow Wolf gathered as much firewood as they could use. Before Larry touched a match to their fire, the hefty half-breed reported, 'I caught the scent of smoke – their fire.'

'Strong or faint?' asked Emma.

'Well ...' he began.

'You or me, we wouldn't've caught a whiff of it,' Larry assured her. 'The Chief's Sioux snoot sniffs farther'n ours could. What d'you say, Chief?'

'A considerable distance ahead of us,' said Slow Wolf. 'But not so far that your plan could not succeed.'

'If *they* make an early start ...' began Emma.

'Uh-huh,' grunted Larry. '*Our* early start'll be all for nothin'. But we're gonna give it a whirl anyway.'

Later, as they squatted close to the fire, warming their insides with the substantial supper cooked by Emma, Larry insisted he would stand the first guard.

'But you must be exhausted,' she protested.

'You won't thank me for remindin' you the goin's harder for a woman,' he said. 'And the Chief'll be standin' the last watch. Let's not forget he had a rougher day than us.'

'I am emotionally drained,' Slow Wolf confessed.

'Sure,' nodded Larry. 'You wiped the blood away and I guess your blubber saved your ribs when they worked you over, but then you were hangin' cat-bait for quite a while before we found you. When Emma relieves me, I'll give her my watch. She'll give it to you when you take over from her.'

'When should we begin seeking their camp?' frowned Slow Wolf.

'You'll rouse us half after three,' said Larry. ''Tween then and the time we finish supper, we'll all get sleep enough to keep us sharp manana.' When they were through eating and Emma reached to the coffee-pot, he took a bottle from his pack. 'The Chief's no dumb Injun, so he's leery of white man's firewater. I ain't about to tie one on, Emma, but spikin' hot coffee with good mash is comfort for the belly on a night so cold. How about you? You temperance?'

He was profoundly impressed when, before replying, she inspected the label.

'Colonel Kemp's bourbon,' she observed. 'A respectable blend. I'll take two fingers with my coffee, thank you.'

Even Slow Wolf still shivered after his two cups of hot and black coffee. The temperature was dropping. They had the fire and some warmth internally, but Emma's teeth chattered when she threw extra wood on the fire and rolled into her blanket. Larry figured he could survive the cold long enough for her to get much-needed sleep, Slow Wolf too, but she was dubious, emphatically so.

'We have to be sensible about this,' she declared, as Larry reached for his rifle and got to his feet. 'Chief, we need each other's body-warmth. Roll into your blanket beside me – *close* beside me.'

'Madam!' gasped Slow Wolf.

'Indians are supposed to be inscrutable,' she dryly remarked to Larry. 'Will you look at his face? Does he think I'm making improper advances?'

'If he was a full-blood, he wouldn't feel this miserable cold like we do,' said Larry. 'It's the white half of him that's chillin' his bones.'

'I couldn't!' Slow Wolf said, aghast.

'Chief, it's hardly likely passions will flare in this damnable cold,' she chided. 'We have to be practical, have to survive, don't we? So do as I say. I need your warmth as much as you'll need mine.'

'Lawrence, I appeal to you ...!' mumbled Slow Wolf.

'I told you – and she told you – why she has to find the Pronto Gang,' said Larry. 'Till her kid brother's back where he belongs, she'll think and act and fight like a man. That's the way she wants it. Meanwhile, we're no help to young Cliff nor to

Stretch if we freeze up here. Better do like she says, Chief.' With a wry grin, he added, 'It'll be somethin' to brag of to your papooses, if you ever sire any.'

'White man speaks with frivolous tongue,' complained Slow Wolf.

Slowly, gingerly, an acutely self-conscious half-Sioux shrouded himself in his blanket and lowered himself to within eighteen inches of the woman. From somewhere under her blanket, she growled a reprimand.

'You're no use *that* far away. *Close* I said, damn it! Or do *I* have to move?'

He rolled close with great reluctance, while Larry patted the picketed horses, pulled his Stetson low and, in his poncho, toted his Winchester clear of the fire. He moved around the overhang, hunkered and, with his gloved hands tucked under his armpits, stared eastward, wondering.

Had the kidnappers fed their victim? Had they thought to throw a blanket over him? Stretch was tough and a survivor. Who'd know that better than his partner of all of twenty years?

'Hold on, stringbean,' he mentally urged. 'You've taken more than one beatin' since they grabbed you. Right now, I guess you're hurtin'. But we've had pain before, right? Sure. A hundred and one times. They might break your body, them stinkin' sonsabitches, but they'll never break your spirit. I ain't givin' up on you, amigo, so don't *you* give up. Sweat it out and wait for me. I'll get to you somehow and, when I do, we'll give 'em no chance at all, no even breaks. They're owlhoot trash and, sure as there's cattle in Texas, we'll make 'em pay for this – in blood.'

A long time for two Texans of such contrasting

personality to stay friends, almost brothers, he reflected. His mind drifted back to the early years, their first meeting. They were the only Texas-born boys of a bunch of feisty southerners descending on a Confederate recruitment depot what seemed a thousand years ago, two kids tall for their tender years, playing hookey from school to scrawl their names on a sheet of paper and swear to be loyal soldiers. Some of the slightly older, slightly bigger enlistees, Missourians, Georgia boys and a couple from Alabama, had dared test the mettle of the young Texans by drawling uncomplimentary remarks about the Lone Star State and its inhabitants. And those kid Texans, who had never set eyes on each other before now, who hadn't even gotten round to trading names, promptly bunched their fists and began defending the fair name of their homestate with gusto.

Some brawl that had been. Their first. They standing back-to-back, hitting hard, sending their adversaries reeling in all directions. By the time the recruiting officer and his noncoms bestirred themselves to quell this disturbance, the young bucks from Texas were the only two still upright.

Were they as good with horses and guns as with their fists, the recruiting officer had demanded? Sassy young Valentine had invited him to try them and, for a quarter-hour thereafter, the salty Texas boys had given an exhibition of fast riding and shooting from the saddle that had the officer and his staff trading knowing grins. The issue was never in doubt; recruits Valentine and Emerson became the youngest troopers of that Texas Cavalry regiment.

Larry remembered now their war years, shot

and shell and all the hell of combat, the near misses, the victories, the judicious retreats, the toughening process – and the years after Appomattox. By then, Stretch was his partner; they were inseparable, the bond had been forged. Restless, they had spent little time in their homestate after the surrender, so then the drifting began, the aimless wandering, the vague hopes that, in their travels, they would find their elusive Utopia, some strife-free region they could hunt and fish at will. Conflict – who needed it? They'd had their fill of blood-letting, were still young and convinced life had better in store for them.

But, of course, they had been wrong. Soon enough, they had enemies more dangerous than the armies of the North had ever been. Their new adversaries were the two-legged predators of the frontiers, thieves and killers of every kind, bandidos, rustlers, horse-thieves, cardsharps, a fine variety of would-be despots. The Lone Star Trouble-Shooters had fought them all, emerging victorious, still surviving, and maybe his hunch was accurate. Why else would a party of outlaws kidnap easy-going Stretch? The outlaw-fighters had made too many enemies, some they'd never seen. Vengeance was the motive, nothing surer.

An all-consuming resolve seized him now. He rejected the prospect of finding his compadre dead, his body bullet-riddled, dangling from a hangrope or blood-drained and dumped in a shallow grave or left unburied for the buzzards. No, damn it, he would find Stretch alive, his beanpole physique abused and in pain, but his spirit surviving. Then he would free him of his bonds, hand him his belted, matched .45s and say, 'Let's get it done.'

And they would get it done, challenge the Pronto Gang – and win.

His eyelids were drooping when the woman came to him. He gave her his watch and trudged back to the fire to flop by the snoring Slow Wolf. Wasn't this something? He grinned wistfully as he drew his blanket up to his chin. The flabby half-breed's snores reminded him of the snores of his partner; that same tuneless, ear-bending sound.

Later, a shivering Emma returned to the fire, dumped more wood on it and bent over the redman.

'Your turn, Chief,' she whispered.

He grunted, got to his moccasined feet, took her rifle and Larry's watch and padded away to listen to the night sounds and scan the terrain east. She rolled into her blanket and nestled close to steady-breathing Larry, choosing his left shoulder as her pillow.

She was still in that position when Slow Wolf killed the fire and woke them.

'I smell their smoke,' he said softly.

'Bueno,' grunted Larry, sitting up. 'Help yourself to Stretch's rifle. It's loaded and, in the saddlebag, you'll find a box of shells. Did you see light?'

'No light,' said Slow Wolf. 'Just the smoke scent.'

'All right,' said Larry. 'Let's load up, saddle up and move out.'

In moonlight broken by the shadows of rocks and timber flanking the trail, they pressed eastward, Slow Wolf leading again. It was almost dawn when their guide's educated nose drew them off the trail and into the timber. They advanced in Indian file for some thirty-five yards before, at Larry's muttered command, reining up and dismounting. Larry and Emma drew their Colts, Slow Wolf readied his borrowed Winchester and, stealthily, they moved on to the near edge of a clearing.

Deserted. No sentry to challenge them. The fire had been smothered with dirt, but not completely, a few wisps of smoke drifting lazily, the scent of which the half-Sioux had caught a long way west of here.

The first sunrays shafted through the trees.

'You're the experts,' said Emma, uncocking and holstering her pistol. 'I see plenty of sign, but you'll read it more clearly than I could.'

Separating, Larry and Slow Wolf moved around slowly, studying hoof and bootprints. Slow Wolf quit the clearing, hurrying in a north-easterly direction to rejoin the trail and read sign.

'Seven horses, includin' my partner's,' Larry called to Emma. 'If I had to make a guess, I'd say they broke camp about the same time we did, maybe a half-hour earlier.'

'Can you see where Stretch slept?' she asked.

'Come take a look,' he invited. She crossed the clearing to kneel beside him. Together, they inspected a strip of soft earth and the rough impression of a long-legged human form. 'Here's where they dumped him – well clear of the fire. Maybe they threw a blanket on him, but I wouldn't take any bets. He must've rolled on his back for a while. That wasn't comfortable for him, so he rolled again. See there? Marks of his hand-ropes show clear, and here, the ankle-ropes.'

'They're sadists,' she said bitterly. 'Would he think to keep flexing his muscles, moving his hands and feet as best he could, to keep his blood circulating?'

'That'd be second nature to him,' he muttered.

Now he bowed his head, staring intently. She followed his example and saw what he saw, the arrow drawn by a finger, pointing east.

FIVE

The Youngest Bandit

Slow Wolf returned to them.

'Their sign is fresher,' he reported. 'I estimate ...'

'Sure,' nodded Larry. 'We ain't so far behind 'em now.'

The redman hunkered to stare at the sign made by the captive.

'Woodville,' he sighed. 'No matter how restricted, he assumes you are searching for him – and leaves a mark.'

'Somethin' else too, just so I'll know his brain still works,' said Larry. With forefinger and thumb and great care, he dislodged something small from the ground a few inches left of the arrow. 'His good luck piece is what he decided to call it.'

He held it on his palm for their appraisal.

'A coin,' frowned Emma. 'A leaden dime.'

'Bent,' observed Slow Wolf.

'He bent it,' Larry told them. 'Change from a dollar, a saloon in Colorado three, maybe four months ago. He didn't catch on it was a fake till we were long gone from that town. Any hombre but Stretch'd gripe about it. He just shrugged and said he'd call it a good-luck piece, stashed it in his hip pocket. Must've still been in that pocket, only pocket he could get into with his hands tied behind him.'

He slipped the leaden dime into a vest pocket.

'Some kind of mental communication, one old friend to another,' Emma said gently. 'You've been together so long, you anticipate each other's movements, can almost read each other's mind.'

'An affinity,' said Slow Wolf.

'Larry, if it's any comfort to you, I believe he *knows* you're on his trail,' she murmured. 'So – he hasn't lost hope.'

'He can add two and two,' said Larry, fishing out his makings. 'Maybe the bandidos think I'm still stuck in the King County jail. Stretch knows better. He'd have remembered Doc Bolger, the one witness that could talk me out of that calaboose – and did.' He rolled and lit a cigarette and stressed the need for greater caution from here on. This was for Emma's benefit; a natural-born tracker of Slow Wolf's calibre already understood. 'No guessin' how close they are to where they're headed. The thing is *we're* closer now. So no fool mistakes. The wind could change. I'm makin' no guesses how soon we'll eat hot chow again.'

'I understand,' said Emma. 'But we have to keep up our strength, so shouldn't we have our last hot meal now? It won't take me long to fix us something.'

'You've seen their sign, Chief,' said Larry. 'Your decision.'

The pudgy man checked the direction of the faint breeze, scanned the available firewood, pondered the question a while and decided this could be their last chance for a hot meal till – who could say? He hunted wood. The horses were kept saddled and Emma was discerning in her choice of provisions taken from the supply lashed to the pack-animal. She fixed strong coffee; Larry again broke out the bottle.

Over that meal, Emma noted Slow Wolf's troubled expression.

'Is he as apprehensive as he looks?' she asked Larry.

'I am, with great difficulty, subduing my mounting fears,' Slow Wolf declared before Larry could answer. 'The prospect of again encountering those blackguards fills me with dread. I am a devout coward who abhors violence, or just the threat of it.'

'I find that hard to believe,' she protested.

'You can believe it – just don't worry about it,' said Larry. 'It ain't a man's fear that matters. It's how he does what he's got to do when the chips're down, meanin' showdown-time. Stretch and me, we've had the chief sidin' us a time or two, and I can tell you he does just fine when it counts the most.'

'Don't confuse that with courage,' Slow Wolf warned her. 'It's dedication to self-preservation. There's a broad distinction, as I'm sure you realize.'

'You believe in protecting yourself,' she smiled. 'Well, fine, good for you. That's every man's right.'

'And he protects himself good,' Larry assured her.

Her mood changed after she poured coffee. They had eaten their fill, a heavier than average breakfast-cum-lunch. Now, for a few moments, she brooded.

'I wonder,' she said, 'what *he's* doing right now – my adventurous brother.'

'At least you know he's safe enough where he's at,' soothed Larry. 'He ain't mixed into no bank raid nor a stagecoach hold-up, because it's for sure he ain't with the main bunch. There was no kid with them six quiet jaspers in the saloon at Kingsville. He had no part in kidnappin' Stretch.'

'Can we be sure the Pronto Gang numbers only a half-dozen?' she countered.

'What're you gettin' at?' he prodded.

'Something puzzles me,' she said. 'If lawmen all over Nevada and the surrounding territories haven't thought of it, they should have. I told you how the gang won its name, how they strike without warning, move fast, loot and kill and then flee just as fast – but could they be *that* fast?'

'If Lawrence isn't confused, *I* most certainly am,' complained Slow Wolf.

'Go ahead, Emma,' urged Larry. 'Make your point.'

'I've read newspaper reports and now I'm pondering the time element,' she said. 'About a year ago, they ambushed a westbound stage in the central Utah area, emptied its strong-box and made a clean getaway, leaving the shotgun guard mortally wounded. Two days later they robbed a bank in a north Nevada town, and, when I say north, I mean far up by the Oregon border. From the middle of the Utah Territory to north Nevada in two days? Tell me how that's possible. Even with fresh horses hidden along their route, could they travel such a distance in *two days*?'

'Unlikely, to say the least,' commented Slow Wolf.

'Hey now,' frowned Larry.

'The gang has to number more than six,' she insisted. 'An even dozen seems more logical. Put it another way. Two groups, the two halves of the same gang.'

'Lawrence, the lady has to be correct,' said Slow Wolf, obviously alarmed again. 'May the Great Spirit protect us! To rescue Woodville and Emma's recalcitrant brother, we may have to contend with ...' he swallowed a lump in his throat along with a gulp of coffee, 'a dozen – or even *more* – assuming some of them remain behind to guard the hideout.'

'Stretch and me, we've gone up against that many before,' Larry said calmly.

'You say "we",' fretted Slow Wolf. 'But "we" does not include poor Woodville.'

'Damn right I'm includin' him,' growled Larry. 'I don't know how I'm gonna do it – too soon for figurin' that – but one thing you can count on. Next time I lay my eyes on the beanpole, I won't be just cuttin' him loose. I'll be handin' him his Colts.'

'That seems too much to hope for,' said Emma. 'But, as you say, it's too soon for devising a strategy.'

Larry drained his cup and said briskly, 'Now we move again. And, from here on, we go quiet.'

'Believe me ...' Slow Wolf shuddered, 'I've no urge to imitate my sire, rest his soul, by screaming Sioux war cries to announce our coming.'

'Somethin' else,' said Larry, as they prepared to move on. 'We can't bet the trail's gonna take us all the way to where they're holed up. If it was that easy, a posse would've found 'em long before now. So stay extra sharp, Chief. Any time from now on, they're apt to break from the trail, or maybe a couple of 'em'll cut a *false* trail. We'd better watch both sides, all three of us.'

'For a cut-off?' asked Emma. 'A route to the hideout?'

'I don't reckon so,' said Larry. 'It mightn't be a trail at all. That's why it's lucky we got the chief along.'

'So much is expected of me,' sighed Slow Wolf.

'You never yet let me down, amigo, and you ain't about to,' declared Larry.

Two hours later, after they had begun another ascent, Slow Wolf called a halt. Larry and Emma stayed mounted, she holding the tie-line of the pack-horse, while the redman swung down and padded into dense mountain brush to their right. Larry began a question; Emma had anticipated it.

'Yes, I've been noticing. For the last mile, no horse-tracks. The drag-riders have been killing sign, maybe with blankets, maybe bundles of brush.'

Larry's confidence in their guide's Indian savvy was justified. Rejoining them some twenty minutes later, Slow Wolf nervously told them, 'The indications are almost imperceptible. Such devilish cunning!'

'What'd you find?' demanded Larry.

'They no longer travel bunched,' said Slow Wolf. 'They stay well separated, but all moving ...'

'East still,' guessed Emma.

'But through brush so *dense*,' fretted Slow Wolf.

'Chief, we only have to follow one of 'em,' muttered Larry. 'They're all headed for the same place.' He gestured to the dun. 'Come on. Fork your critter. Emma, you stay close behind him. Let me have that tie-rope. This time I'm tag-rider.'

They veered from the trail and into the thick brush. Now they would climb again, but with considerable difficulty.

At 2 pm of this day, captive and his captors came to the end of the long ascent through dense brush, reaching level ground, but not much of it. As the horsemen grouped again, Stretch used his eyes. The cliff-face directly ahead seemed impenetrable, its surface cluttered with a confusion of high country growth.

'Now you'll savvy how safe we're hid,' Farley Cross told him. 'You'll know what no search-party ever found out.'

'But that doesn't bother us, Emerson,' grinned Werris. 'Once inside the hideout, you'll be there the rest of your life – which won't last long after Jethro gets here.'

What followed keenly interested the captive despite his predicament and the question constantly gnawing at his mind – would he ever get out of this fix alive, live to talk of it?

Werris unsheathed his rifle, walked his mount straight to a section of the cliff's base and thrust the butt of the weapon into thick foliage. At once, Stretch heard the thud of it. Four times Werris struck with his rifle-butt. The thudding sounds seemed to echo, or maybe that was Stretch's imagination playing tricks, but of one thing he was certain; Werris was hitting hard timber.

A few moments later, a square section swung

inward to the accompaniment of subdued squealing. Like a big gate, Stretch observed, and high enough for riders to pass through.

'Red, time to oil those hinges again,' he heard Werris say.

Ivers took the pinto's rein and led its helpless rider into the opening, following the disappearing Werris. They were in a tunnel. Stretch, seeing daylight at its end, calculated it to be forty feet long. And a natural tunnel at that. Pickaxes hadn't dug it through the the mountainside; its roof curved and neither side showed shoring timbers.

He had noticed the tall redhead. Without glancing back past the horsemen, he knew the redhead was resecuring the entrance. The clang of metal on metal suggested an iron bar was being dropped into place. From outside, that camouflaged timber door could never be battered down; only dynamite could destroy it. Through the tunnel and into the sunlit floor of the crater moved the riders, Stretch warily scanning the layout, the shacks and tents, all flimsy except for the bigger cabin, log-based and plank-roofed. The rock fireplaces surprised him. Didn't these owlhooters care if their smoke was sighted from afar? But then he raised his eyes and answered his own question. The slopes of the great circle rose to towering heights. They could be climbed, he realized. But the outer walls of this crater? Probably not. Too steep. So the Pronto Gang had devised the best of all hideaways.

Huber reappeared when Werris and the others were dismounting by a pole corral.

'Got yourself a prisoner,' he observed.

'Recognize him?' grinned Werris.

The big redhead squinted at the pinto's slumped rider.

'Who ...?'

'Emerson is who!' chuckled Werris. 'The great Valentine's cooped in a county jail and we got Emerson!'

'For Tragg to play with,' breathed Huber, baring his teeth. 'By Judas, he'll sure thank you for fetchin' Emerson alive.'

'I could near throw up,' remarked Murquette, 'thinkin' of what Jethro'll do to him.'

'On my figurin', Jethro's bunch should get in pretty soon,' said Werris. 'Meanwhile, we keep Emerson trussed, but fed good.' He jerked a thumb. 'Carl, dump him in that shelter by the north wall.'

Ivers and another man untied Stretch's hands and feet, hauled him to the ground and, while two others stood by with cocked Colts levelled, retied him. He was then dragged across the flat ground by his feet and tossed into a tent, its canvas ripped and frayed.

'How'd you make out?' Huber asked when all the horses were corralled. 'How good a bundle did you take from the Galesburg Bank?'

'Haven't tallied it, but I figure twenty thousand or thereabouts,' said Werris. He proffered a bulging sack. 'We'd better abide by Jethro's rules. Stash this in his cabin right away and don't get curious about how much it holds.' As Huber made to move off, he asked, 'The Kid behavin' himself?'

'Givin' no trouble,' said Huber. 'He'll do, Sid. Knows how to follow orders, got to give him that.'

'Cy!' Werris called to Aberlain. 'Climb up and

take over from the Reno Kid. I got a special chore for him!'

Responding to Werris's beckoning, seeing Aberlain begin climbing, Cliff Dane started down with mixed feelings. He was curious that the Werris group had returned with a seventh man, a prisoner. Why would the Pronto Gang bring a prisoner to the hideout? Better keep his curiosity to himself, he decided. None of his new companeros took kindly to too many questions.

Werris was shaving by the spring dead centre of the crater floor when he reached him.

'Howdy,' he nodded.

'Red tells me you've been doin' fine,' remarked Werris. 'Spellin' him at lookout duty, handlin' your share of the cookin'.'

'Like I told the Boss,' said Cliff, 'I'm good at followin' orders.'

'Got a mighty important order for you now, Kid,' said Werris. 'Now who d'you suppose Carl and Elmo stashed in that old tent?' Cliff shrugged. 'Can't guess, huh? Well, maybe you never heard of him, but Jethro sure has, and my hunch is Jethro'll skin him alive – with pleasure.'

'Who is he?' asked Cliff.

'Ever hear of the Texas Trouble-Shooters?'

'Yeah, sure. Who hasn't?'

'That one's Stretch Emerson. Heard Jethro talk of *him*, right?'

Cliff managed to stay impassive.

'Right, Sid. It was Emerson killed the Boss's brother.'

'When Jethro gets back, Emerson'll be a dead man,' grinned Werris. 'But not right away. A bullet in his head'd be too quick, too merciful to

Jethro's way of thinkin'. It'll be somethin' to see, won't it? Jethro pleasurin' himself? Believe me, Kid, he'll give that big hero pain, a lot of it, before he finally finishes him off.'

'That'll sure be somethin' to see,' muttered Cliff.

'You're gonna be Emerson's special guard,' said Werris. 'He stays tied, but you feed him regular. He's got to be strong enough to take all Jethro's gonna give him. Jethro wouldn't have it any other way.'

'Okay,' nodded Cliff.

'Remember now, you never untie him,' stressed Werris. 'I'm makin' him your responsibility – provin' I got confidence in you. Feed him with a fork or a spoon, savvy?'

'Savvy,' said Cliff.

'What's on that fire?' asked Werris.

'Just a pan of beans, some coffee,' said Cliff.

'Go feed him now,' ordered Werris. 'But don't get careless, Kid. Even tied up, he's liable to try anything, like kickin' your legs from under you.'

'I won't take any chances with him,' promised Cliff.

Prone on the tent's dirt floor, Stretch was using his eyes again. Nothing in here. Empty, except for him. He was hungry again, but his ribs had stopped aching and, so far, he had suffered no head damage; he could still think, observe, listen – and hope.

So the boss of this outfit, name of Jethro Tragg, thought he had a blood debt to settle and, as Werris gloatingly predicted, would butcher him slowly. Well, slow was better than fast, all circumstances considered. The longer he stayed alive, even in agony, the more time he bought for his partner. And Larry would need plenty of *that* – damn right – a lot of time, to find another way into this robbers' roost. Forget about the great door and its iron bar. It could only be opened from the inside and only if returning raiding parties signalled their arrival, the four spaced blows from a rifle-butt. So Larry would have to do it the hard way.

His own chances of getting free? He studied his canvas prison again. Something sharp would be mighty useful. Rub his wrist-ropes against it till the strands frayed and parted. Good idea, but there was nothing here, sharp or otherwise. A thought occurred to him. Outlaws aren't temperance. If a bottle had been discarded, smashed some time ago maybe right here in this tent, he might find a piece of it in the dirt floor. Well, that would be something to occupy him, but not right away. Approaching footsteps. He was about to have company.

He was surprised when the young man, the very young man, entered toting a tin plate, spoon and steaming cup. The Colt with its staghorn grips was jammed into a tied-down holster, he noted, so maybe this was some kid gunslinger.

'Eatin' time for you,' muttered Cliff.

'Much obliged, boy,' Stretch said softly. 'Maybe you don't like being called "boy" so – you got a name?'

'They call me the Reno Kid,' growled Cliff. He hunkered, spooned up beans. 'Just shuddup and eat, trouble-shooter.'

Stretch was only too happy to do that. When the plate was empty and his young guard holding the cup to his mouth, he sipped and remarked, 'Kind of young for ridin' with these owlhooters, ain't you?'

'I'm as ornery as any Pronto rider, and you better

believe it,' Cliff said defensively.

'You called me trouble-shooter,' Stretch recalled after another mouthful of coffee. 'Guess you know me, huh?'

'Yeah, sure,' sneered Cliff. 'You're Emerson, one of those famous show-off Texans that butt into what's none of their business.'

'Yup,' grunted Stretch, drinking again. 'Keeps happenin', you know? Joke's on us, Reno. My partner and me, we never went lookin' for a run-in with bandidos. It ain't what we want. It's just somethin' keeps happenin' to us.'

'It was an unlucky day for you, the day you gunned down the Boss's brother,' said Cliff. 'It's gonna cost you your life, tall feller, but a lot of pain first, they tell me.'

'Ever hear of Larry or me backshootin' a thief – or one that wasn't packin' iron?' asked Stretch. 'Them we've killed, they've been doin' their doggonedest to kill us. We got a lot of scars to prove that, Reno.'

'That's what *you* say,' jibed Cliff. He set the empty cup on the plate with the spoon and withdrew a pace, studying the prisoner. 'By damn, you don't look so tough right now, Emerson.'

'Don't *feel* tough,' Stretch replied with a rueful grin. 'Ain't just that I'm hogtied. Like you can see, they beat on me a time or two since they stole me out of Kingsville.'

'You and Valentine're supposed to be too rough for any that crowd you,' said Cliff. 'No matter how many. Sid and the boys, just six of 'em, proved that's a dumb lie.'

'Think they faced up to me fair and square, do you?' prodded Stretch. He shook his head wearily.

'No, young feller, not so you'd notice. They played it sneaky, bought me a drink, slipped somethin' in it. I was dead on my feet when I made it back to the hotel, near passin' out. That's the only way they could take me. It had to be a sure thing, no risks for 'em.'

'I don't care a hoot in hell about …' began Cliff.

'Just somethin' for you to think about,' shrugged Stretch. 'You've thrown in with these bandidos, so you might's well savvy the kind of skunks you're runnin' with now.' As Cliff turned to leave him, he cunningly enquired, 'You sure they're *your* kind?'

'Nice try, trouble-shooter, but it won't work,' Cliff jeered at him. 'Sid's made you my responsibility, hear? I feed and guard you, and I aim to guard you good. I'll be right outside and stayin' plenty alert. Even if you could break loose from those ropes, I'd make sure you don't run. And I'm a sure shot. You'd get a bullet in a foot.'

'I wouldn't like that,' Stretch said mildly.

'You sure wouldn't.'

With that, the youth slouched out. He was alone again and with new ideas coming to him. The Reno Kid warranted some thought. He wasn't forgetting the smooth face of his guard nor the gruff speech, tough talk of an obviously rebellious spirit. Just how young was he? Hell, he didn't look a month older than seventeen, if you could judge by looks.

Could this boy stand by and watch him tortured without protest? Well, of course, the kid didn't dare protest. But would he enjoy the scene? Stretch had strong doubts and a new hope. Maybe he had found a chink in the armour of the Pronto Gang. The kid had to be their latest recruit, and was he as ready as the other outlaws believed? Or was he the weak link, the one member of the band he could work on, soften up, even persuade to help him escape?

'That mightn't be fair,' he reflected. 'How could he help me without them knowin' it? I could get him killed.'

He leaned backward, dug his fingers into the soft earth and began prodding and probing. Just one sliver of glass was all he needed, or an embedded rock. It didn't have to be sharp. Rubbed against its rough, hard surface, his wrist-ropes would eventually weaken, and fray. But how long was eventually, how much time did he have?

His efforts were unsuccessful; he found nothing.

By sundown, at which time Cliff Dane was again feeding the prisoner, Larry checked the sky and decided against advancing further.

'We talk soft from here on,' he cautioned.

The hunters had found no clearing, just a hollow in the brushy slope of a size to accommodate three humans and four horses. All around, the brush was dense, seemingly impenetrable. They knew better of course. Their quarry had fanned out in pairs and passed this way; Slow Wolf was in no doubt about the signs he had read, indications that might be unnoticed by a white man, twisted foliage, strands gashed by spurs, patches of brush askew, bent by the weight of a hoof.

He, Larry and Emma were also aware of the great bulk farther east, the high mountainside.

'We may well be close,' winced the half-breed, as they huddled together to eat from unheated cans. 'I warmly agree, Lawrence my friend, we should not raise our voices.'

'My money's on the mountain,' muttered Larry. 'Maybe it's flat-topped and maybe that's their roost.'

'So, somewhere along the near base, we should find a track?' asked Emma.

'Game-trail perhaps,' suggested Slow Wolf. 'If that's their route to the hideout, I imagine it winds and, in places, is extremely steep.'

'The thing is, we can climb it if they can,' said Larry. 'But it's for sure they post lookouts, so we'll have to go careful.' He munched and swallowed, aimed a thoughtful glance at the horses and remarked, 'Only safe way might be to leave our animals here and try it on our own feet.'

'We'd make less noise that way,' Emma agreed. 'So ...' She leaned closer, the better to study his expression, 'are we now assuming they've reached – or almost reached – their base?'

'The Chief checked ahead an hour ago,' he reminded her. 'If they were nightcampin' again, he'd know.'

After that cold food, they craved hot coffee, but waxed stoic. No use fooling themselves. If they believed themselves to be closer now to their destination, they had to acknowledge the obvious danger of using a fire. As Emma said, with a shrug of resignation, 'We've come too far to foolishly betray our presence.'

Slow Wolf could get by with a swig of water from Larry's canteen. Emma begged for and was given a stiff shot of rye. Larry poured the same quantity for himself, and, when he had downed it, warned, 'Tonight'll be rougher for us – no fire to warm us.'

'Chief, I envy you your excess fat,' sighed Emma.

'Only one way we'll make it through the night,'

declared Larry. 'Stay bunched, close together under our blankets. If one of us sits guard atop this hollow, he'll freeze for sure.'

'It's my feeling our quarry don't suspect they've been tracked, certainly not this far,' mumbled Slow Wolf.

'I got the same feelin',' nodded Larry. 'Anyway, I can count on an old friend.' He gestured to his sorrel. 'If we're in danger from snoopers, he'll let me know.'

'I've noticed how quickly you wake,' said Emma.

'It's the life they've led, Lawrence and poor Woodville,' Slow Wolf gloomily informed her. 'Sad, the irony of it all. Two such pleasant, amiable nomads, admirable fellows, doomed to travel in the shadow of the Grim Reaper, peril, tension and the threat of violence forever dogging their trail.'

'Redman speaks with loose tongue,' chided Larry. 'Much obliged, but the beanpole and me can do our own gripin' when we got a mind to.'

'It is a tragedy,' insisted Slow Wolf. 'Your bravado becomes you, but you know I speak only the truth.'

Abruptly, Larry changed the subject.

'How about when it's finished?' he asked Emma.

'Finished?' she frowned.

'I mean after we're through, when you and your proddy brother are headed for home, when I've patched Stretch's wounds and him and me get back to driftin',' he said. 'Listen, Emma honey, we're gonna win. If I wasn't sure we could finish what we started, I wouldn't have brought you this far. Now how about the kid? Will this do it for him, teach him a lesson, make him mend his ways?'

'You don't intend treating him as you'd treat

any other outlaw – turn him in to the law?' she challenged. 'Larry, what if he's already ridden with these bandits, taken part in armed robbery?'

'He's no real outlaw,' he said gruffly. 'He's a fool kid *playin'* outlaw. By now, he could be scared near out of his mind.'

'If that's so, maybe he'll benefit from the experience,' she said. 'I have to say it'd be a welcome change at Rocking D, Cliff settling down, helping Uncle Tim and me run the spread, no more wild streak.'

'How you must have worried, dear Emma,' Slow Wolf sympathized.

'Of course I've worried,' she murmured. 'I still worry, but I keep that to myself. A fretting woman would be no help to Larry. He has more than enough on his mind already.'

'You're some tough lady.' Larry said it softly but vehemently, meaning every word. 'Promise me somethin', Emma.'

'If I can,' she offered.

'You won't stay single forever – that wouldn't be natural,' he opined. 'When the time comes that some hombre takes a shine to you and talks of marriage, don't settle for second-best, okay? He has to be a good man, brain as well as muscle, the kind who'll treat you like you deserve and stay loyal. You be damn particular, hear?'

She looked away from him, a woman with her own ideas about men, especially one man. Could this one man handle such a complication at this critical time, she was thinking? The worst, the most potentially disastrous thing she could do would be to speak her mind, to tell Larry Valentine exactly how she felt about Larry Valentine.

Emma Dane was nobody's fool, and proved it by smiling, shrugging and assuring both her companions, 'You needn't be concerned on my account. When I think of marriage, that's how my mind works. A woman must be particular and choose with care, if she hopes to be happy.'

'I'll hold you to that,' warned Larry. 'Couple years from now, if Stretch and me find our way to Rockin' D, I wouldn't want to find you stuck with a husband that ain't worthy of you. I'd get plenty mad, understand?'

'I understand perfectly,' she replied. 'And now, if you'll wipe that troubled look off your supposed-to-be-inscrutable face, Chief, hadn't we better wrap ourselves in the blankets and try to sleep? Tomorrow is another day – and the Lord alone knows what's in store for us.'

This night, the odd trio survived the intense cold by huddling close, Emma wedged between two compulsive nomads, one white, one swarthy. If the men were uneasy, she certainly wasn't.

They slept.

But, a good distance from the mountain, where the Hoolahan expedition was nightcamped, it was too early for calling it a day or posting guards. Were it not for the moonlight and the keen eyes of the unkempt Paiute Jake, the big force might still have been travelling. Now they were camped in a sizeable clearing in a forest, warming themselves by cookfires and consuming a delayed supper, every man ravenous.

Well separated from their bumptious leader, Agents Casey and Zimmerman were eating with an inquisitive Deputy Falk.

SIX
Sting of the Lash

The two Pinkertons, old cronies, mutually decided the curiosity of the blunt-speaking deputy should be dealt with diplomatically; considerable discretion was required.

'Your bull-voiced boss,' Falk said before jabbing his fork into a chunk of stewed beef. 'He *really* a big shot of the Pinkerton outfit?'

'A senior officer,' nodded Casey. 'His classification is Chief Investigator.'

'Veteran of the business,' said Zimmerman.

'He gets results?' Falk sounded dubious.

'Well, certainly,' Zimmerman assured him.

'I guess you can't always tell from lookin' and listenin',' frowned the deputy, after masticating and swallowing. 'Me now, I've been lookin' and listenin', studyin' his style and …'

'You aren't impressed,' guessed Zimmerman.

'First impressions,' Casey warned. 'You can get a lot of wrong ideas from first impressions.'

'So maybe I'm wrong, maybe he ain't a blowhard and a jackass,' shrugged Falk.

'Perish the thought,' said Casey, hiding a grin, trading winks with his colleague.

'Dan's had a lot of success,' Zimmerman said loyally.

'It's no new name to me – Special Agent Daniel P. Hoolahan,' confided Falk. 'I've read of him in more'n one newspaper.'

'Cases investigated and closed by good old Dan, I'm sure,' said Casey.

'Nope.' Falk shook his head emphatically. 'The couple times I read of him, there were these two hot-shot drifters, Texans, that beat him to it. Heard of Valentine and Emerson, have you?'

'Deputy, do us all a favour,' begged Zimmerman. 'Don't mention those names in Dan's hearing. Speak softly of them.'

'You know who I mean,' persisted Falk. 'The Texas Trouble-Shooters? They've fought more badmen than the newspapers can keep count of.'

'We know 'em.' Casey nodded guiltily. 'Confidentially, we like 'em.'

'Great guys,' enthused Zimmerman, but almost in a whisper. 'A couple of real pistols, those two.'

'And it's true,' declared Falk. 'It was them nailed some of the bandidos Hoolahan was huntin'. They handled all the dangerous chores. Hoolahan, he just kind of took delivery of 'em after Valentine and his buddy'd caught 'em.'

'It doesn't happen that way every time,' said Zimmerman. 'But, yes, it has happened.'

'Much to Dan's disapproval,' explained Casey. 'So, you see, it's only natural he resents their crazy luck. And that's what it is, Deputy. Crazy luck, the way Larry and Stretch nail a bunch of criminals one jump ahead of him.'

'Me and Jeff don't resent 'em,' retorted Falk. 'Every bandit bunch they round up, they're savin' us county lawmen a big chore, a lot of ridin' and trackin' and maybe a shootin' showdown. Hell, if them Texans ever showed up in Alvarado, me and Jeff'd shake their hands and treat 'em to the best booze Dick Quilley stocks.'

'I don't believe Dan'll ever do that,' grinned Zimmerman.

'I guess we have to listen to this,' sighed Casey. Having satisfied his appetite, Hoolahan was rising to address his aides, the Alvarado lawmen and the volunteers. 'Here comes another speech. We'd best heed our leader's words.'

'Give me one good reason why,' muttered Zimmerman.

It was a stirring address calculated to fire his force with the urge to do battle with the Pronto Gang – in Hoolahan's opinion. For fifteen minutes, while the volunteers kept right on eating, while many of them traded bemused glances, the boss-Pinkerton held forth on the subject of the desperadoes they sought to bring to justice, the depredations of said desperadoes, the proud record of the Pinkerton Agency, the need for his volunteers to maintain cool nerves, a keen eye and a readiness to ignore the risks and give of their best when, as he had no doubt, their scout would locate the hideout, when he, Daniel P. Hoolahan, would lead the charge into the outlaw stronghold.

On that note, he finished his speech. The Alvarado men drank coffee – in silence.

'What the hell did he expect?' Zimmerman whispered to Casey. 'Applause?'

'Probably thought some jasper'd start singing the Battle Hymn Of The Republic,' said Casey.

In the morning, Larry was first to stir. He opened

his eyes to the first sunrays and sat up. As he began freeing himself from the blankets, Slow Wolf and the woman came awake. And then, just as Emma began rising, they heard the subdued hoofbeats and a sound now very familiar to them, the thick brush disturbed by horses.

Larry's reaction was automatic. He glanced at Emma, held a finger to his lips and nodded to Slow Wolf. They stood quiet, waiting. Not till the horsemen had passed some forty yards north of the hollow and moved on eastward did the flabby half-breed stir; he pulled a fast and soundless disappearing trick. Emma came close to Larry. He bent to permit her to put her mouth to his ear.

'If we're going to bet on this,' she whispered, 'I'm betting the other half of the gang has returned.'

'My bet too,' he said softly. 'And we needn't fret about Slow Wolf. When he gets back to us – they'll never spot him, count on that – we'll know if my hunch is right. The hideout's atop or somewhere around that mountain.'

As quietly as possible, she took food from the packs, just three cans of pork and beans and some jerky, strips of dried beef. Larry opened two cans. They ate on their feet and, thirty minutes later, when their pudgy compadre came padding back to them, he opened the other can. If Slow Wolf was excited, it had to be conceded he was striving for the inscrutability of his Sioux forebears. His voice didn't shake when, after getting some of his food down, he reported seeing six horsemen enter the mountain.

'*Enter* it?' frowned Emma.

'I do not wonder that search-parties of white men have failed to locate the secret entrance,' he muttered. 'Such fiendish cunning. But, of course, nature aided them. A geological freak.'

'Make sense,' urged Larry.

'Better I show you the place,' insisted Slow Wolf. 'Were I to attempt to describe what I saw, it would only confuse you. We can safely move on now, but only a short distance by horseback. There are bound to be lookouts atop the crater. That's what it has to be, my friends. A crater. The mountain is hollow.'

'Right,' said Larry. 'We'll ...'

'Pack our gear, saddle up and move on,' said Emma.

'Ain't that just like a woman?' Larry grouched to Slow Wolf. 'Takin' the words right out of my mouth?'

They made haste to ready the horses and, in a matter of minutes, their overweight ally was leading Larry and Emma east again, Emma electing to take charge of the pack-animal. At a certain point, Slow Wolf called a halt, insisting they should now proceed afoot and cautiously. As little disturbance of the brush as they could manage; lookouts have sharp eyes.

He led them to where the thick growth ended and, there, they half-knelt, staying close, surveying the level ground directly ahead, the heavily foliaged face of the mountain. Very quietly, the half-breed directed their attention to a particular section.

'Transplanted mountain growth,' he whispered. 'Only an experienced observer could note the discrepancy.'

'Tell that plainer,' begged Larry.

'He means the plants growing there don't match

the outgrowths left and right of it,' offered Emma.

'I presume it to be of logs,' said Slow Wolf. 'Mud has been packed against this side of it and foliage replanted so that, given time, it would be completely concealed. It is a door, Lawrence. The leader of the six struck it with a rifle-butt four times, and that was obviously a signal. That whole section opened inward. I heard a creak of metal hinges and, as they filed through, I realized they were entering a natural tunnel – even glimpsed daylight beyond.'

'When the last rider passed through …' began Larry.

'The door was closed – and barred,' said Slow Wolf.

'The hell of it is *we* can't get in that way,' scowled Larry.

'We know the signal, but daren't use it,' complained Emma. 'Unless there are more than a dozen of them, a third group expected to return – and we can't depend on that.'

Larry was scanning the base of the mountain. He stared upward and grimaced. No hope of scaling that rocky, thick-brushed cliff-face, not on this side anyway; it was practically perpendicular.

'We'll move back to where we left the horses,' he muttered.

'Are you planning …?' began Emma.

'Gettin' an idea,' he said, as they retreated. 'It'll have to work. It's the only way I can think of. Hell, if the beanpole's still alive, I got to reach him. Ain't gonna be easy, but I got to try it.'

When they returned to the horses, he confided his plan while detaching his and his partner's lariats and the rope recovered from the scene of Slow Wolf's close call with a pain-crazed cougar. With cord, he improvised a sling for his Winchester; he also secured the buckle of his partner's buscadero shellbelt with filled holsters and hooked it over his left shoulder. Slow Wolf listened solemnly, Emma with her eyes widening.

'It could be an impossible task,' she protested. 'And, if you fell …'

'I just told you,' Larry said impatiently. 'I aim to follow the base round to the north side and find a part I *can* climb.'

'Laden with …' began Slow Wolf.

'Just my long gun and Stretch's Colts,' he said, 'the rope and a little jerky. Like to take my field-glasses along, but that'd be extra weight, a canteen too. Look, I don't fool myself it's gonna be easy – or quick. Could take me most of this day to get up there.'

'While we wait in sight of that camouflaged entrance,' frowned Emma, 'unable to get inside and help you unless you can reach and open it for us.'

'Might be me let's you in,' said Larry. 'Might be kid brother Cliff. Too early to guess, and it depends on how he feels about everything, you know? Emma, you got my word I'll protect the kid as best I can, but I got to think of Stretch too.'

'We will be waiting, Lawrence,' Slow Wolf promised. 'No matter how long it takes.'

'Remember now, you fetch the rifles and all the spare shells you can carry, just them and your blankets,' said Larry. 'It's likely you'll be waitin' there all night.' Hefting three coils, the two lariats and the extra rope, he got to his feet. 'That's all. I got to move now.'

'May the Great Spirit ...' began Slow Wolf.

'Yeah, muchas gracias,' nodded Larry. ''Be seein' you.'

He traded brief glances with Emma before hurrying away. She matched stares with the pudgy redman a moment, heaved a sigh and began taking extra ammunition from the fourth horse's pack.

'I too fear for him, and not for the first time, Emma dear,' he said gently. 'There have been – difficult situations – many times when I have doubted they could survive, my Texan brothers. But they *do* survive. Their warrior instincts never fail them.'

'All right,' she nodded. 'I'll try to be as optimistic as you, Chief. And now *we'd* better move to our position.'

Some thirty minutes later, having worked his way around to the crater's north outer wall, Larry scanned the heights he meant to reach and the surface he must climb. He decided to search no further. This section would have to be it. Much of it was steep. He would certainly need to throw a loop over outcrops, make hand-over-hand ascents in several places. The going would be rough – and hazardous – but now he was feeling lucky.

He began climbing.

The return of the boss-outlaw and five other members of the Pronto Gang was heard by the captive in the flimsy shelter over by the base of the north slope. Cliff Dane rose from the box he had placed a few yards from the tent flaps and waved to Jethro Tragg's companions, five as homicidal as they who had ridden with Werris. Tragg grinned his way, showing his yellowing buck-teeth, unslung a sack, tossed it to Ivers and asked Werris, 'How's our fourteenth man comin' along?'

'Comin' along just fine, Jethro,' grinned Werris. 'On guard duty right now.'

Tragg dismounted, frowning. The leader, the planner and decision-maker of the gang was a hawk-nosed six-footer of rangy physique. Like his shoulder-length mane, the flowing moustache and long beard were light brown. The eyes were cold grey under the bushy brows that curled up at their extremities. The range clothes were shabby and filthy. Jethro Tragg cared nought for his looks, nor for hygiene. The sack thrown to Ivers, who now toted it to the larger cabin for storage, contained the loot from his latest coup, a stage robbery. When he decided to pay shares of the fortune stowed in his cabin to his men, when he was ready to head for California and a life of ease, then would he rid himself of his whiskers, buy fine clothes and present a respectable façade to people unaware of the source of his wealth.

'I ain't blind, Sid,' he growled. 'The Kid's settin' over there right where I can see him. He ain't up top takin' a turn at guard duty.'

'Farley's on lookout,' said Werris. 'The Kid's guardin' a prisoner.'

'A what?' challenged Tragg.

'A smart-ass Texan you ordered every man to look out for,' chuckled Werris. 'Emerson, Jethro. We got him for you, sneaked him out of a burg called Kingsville.' As Tragg bared his teeth, he added, 'And we needn't fret about the other one.

Valentine's sweatin' in the King County jail. So Emerson's all yours, just like you wanted.'

'By Judas!' cried Tragg, his eyes dilating. 'This is what I've hungered for!' He bellowed to Cliff. 'Drag him out, Kid!'

Cliff didn't dare hesitate. He rose, moved into the tent and grasped the prisoner's wrist-ropes.

'So the time's come, huh boy?' muttered Stretch, as Cliff began dragging him out.

'Shuddup, I got nothin' to say to you,' mumbled Cliff.

He hauled Stretch across the crater floor to dump him before Tragg, who loosed a wild, ragged laugh. At once, Stretch's brow was gashed. Tragg kicked hard. His head rang, but he was well and truly conscious when Werris raised him to an awkward squatting posture for his leader's avid appraisal.

'Yeah, you're Emerson – you no-account sonofabitch!' gasped Tragg. 'You're the one robbed me of Ruben – best brother a man ever had!'

Stretch looked up to study the unprepossessing face of a crazed killer. And could not conceal his contempt.

'Your brother, Tragg,' he muttered. 'And a thief like you. You say I killed him? I ain't doubtin' that. But he'd have had a bead on me.'

'You killed Ruben and – oh, glory – it's gonna cost you!' leered Tragg. He made no move to draw a pistol. Stretch would have been surprised if he had. Turning to his men, Tragg said elatedly, 'I ain't gonna rush this. Reckon I'll give myself three, maybe four days of pleasure, workin' him over. But startin' *now*! Little exercise'll give me an appetite!'

He barked orders and Werris and the others were quick to obey. Cliff felt his gorge rise, but somehow managed to hide his revulsion. Shovels were fetched along with two logs. Post-holes were dug and the logs rammed into them upright and made firm. Two men then untied the captive while the others drew and aimed pistols to deter him from running. Stretch was raised and his hands secured again, this time to the upright logs so that his long arms were outstretched. Aberlain was sent to fetch a whip, while two men tore at Stretch's upper garments, stripping him to the waist.

'This is for Ruben – and this is only the start, hero!' guffawed Tragg, reaching for the whip.

Stretch clenched his teeth and made himself a promise. He would suffer this agony in silence. Not one yelp, not one whimper would this human buzzard hear from him. The hell with Tragg and all his no-good crew. He wouldn't give them that satisfaction.

Tragg yelled obscenities as he swung the whip. The first cut felt to Stretch like a red-hot branding iron laid across his back. His face contorted, but he stayed close-mouthed as Tragg lashed at him again and again. He wasn't counting the strokes, wasn't fainting either, just keeping his teeth clenched, taking as much punishment as his torturer could inflict. In a daze of agony, he supposed Tragg would keep swinging that whip till he was breathless.

During the tall man's torment, Cliff was building a cigarette, hoping his hands weren't trembling and covertly studying Werris, Big Red Huber, Carl Ivers, all the men watching their bestial boss in action. All but Farley Cross, up there atop the west wall, enjoyed a close view of what the lash was doing to the Texan's back, criss-crossing it with livid weals. He read their faces and saw no compassion, no vague hint of disgust. Most of them grinned. Ivers, Murquette and three who had returned with Tragg were chuckling.

Oh, hell. What kind of men, if such they could be called, were these? Bold, brave outlaws? Fearless bandidos – the kind he had yearned to join? He thought of Rocking D and the sister he had accused of bullying him and, with a chill in his belly, wondered if he would ever see the old place again. It didn't seem likely. He was a Tragg man now and there was only one hero here, only one worthy of respect – the one suffering at Tragg's hands.

Tiring at last, Tragg dropped the whip. He stood panting a while, catching his breath. When next he spoke, his voice was raspy.

'Take him down, hogtie him again.' His gaze switched to Cliff. 'You, Kid, after you dump him back in that tent, hustle to my shack and fetch the medicine box. You'll find some kinda balm. Smear it on his back. I don't want for him to take blood poison and die – not yet. And, when we eat, *he* eats, savvy? He's gotta be alive enough to feel more pain.'

'When's he gettin' it again, Jethro?' Werris asked as Ivers and Aberlain began untying the tall man.

'Tomorrer,' leered Tragg. He moved to a fire, bent to draw out an eighteen inch long piece of wood, raised it and studied its blazing front end.

'Tomorrer I burn him some. Might start with his eyes. He ain't gonna need 'em no more anyway.'

This reply won approving laughter from his cohorts. Ivers and Aberlain had finished resecuring the prisoner's wrists and ankles. They let him fall face-down. Cliff went to him, grasped the back of his pants-belt and made slow work of half-toting, half-dragging him back to the tent.

When he lowered Stretch, his scalp crawled. He couldn't believe this man was still conscious, capable of speech, but he was! All Stretch said was, 'You enjoy it – like them trail-trash did?'

'Uh – lie quiet,' sighed Cliff. 'I got to put somethin' on them whip-cuts.'

A few minutes later, finding himself alone in the cabin where Tragg slept, where the proceeds of countless robberies were stored, he made for the tin box on a shelf to the rear. En route, he darted a glance at the generous liquor supply, all the bottles stacked on another shelf. Would one of those flat pint bottles be missed? Hell, who kept tally? He stowed one inside his shirt, took the medical kit down and moved out again.

In the tent, with Cliff hunkered beside him, smearing ointment on his lacerations, Stretch softly enquired, 'Anybody else close enough to hear?'

'Just shuddup.'

'I asked you a question, boy.'

'All right. They can't hear us.'

'Bueno. I got another question. You still think it was a smart notion, throwin' in with that scum out there?'

Cliff finished his chore, wiped his hands on his Levis, capped the jar and returned it to the box.

He lifted Stretch half-upright, produced the bottle, darted a furtive glance over his shoulder and pulled the cork.

'You need ...' he began.

'Ain't that the truth,' said Stretch, opening his mouth. He swigged whiskey till the bottle was only two-thirds full, then closed his mouth. Cliff replaced the cork, hesitated a moment, then burrowed a hole into which he inserted the bottle. 'Right kindly of you, kid.'

'You can maybe get at it,' mumbled Cliff. 'I don't know. One thing's sure, I can't tie your hands in front of you.'

'How the hell'd you get mixed up with these skunks?' demanded Stretch. 'Where you from?'

'None of your business,' said Cliff. 'A long way from here.'

'Think this is where you belong?' challenged Stretch. 'You havin' a good time?'

'You ask too many questions,' complained Cliff.

'How about a smoke?' pleaded Stretch. Cliff rolled and lit a cigarette and nudged it into the side of his mouth. He inhaled and puffed gratefully. 'If I don't ask questions, how'll I know if any of you – maybe just one of you – rates an even break when the time comes?'

'When – *what* time comes?' blinked Cliff.

'Take a chance,' Stretch urged himself. 'You got any choice? This proddy young'un ain't like the others.'

'You know what time I mean,' he muttered. 'Pronto Gang keeps workin', so posses keep lookin' for this place. You think no passel of tin stars'll ever find that log gate? Has to happen, kid. Could happen soon, maybe while I'm still alive. So I better know about you and what you tell me better be the truth.'

'I don't have to tell you anything,' blustered Cliff.

'Ridden with 'em yet?' prodded Stretch. 'Done any killin'?' Cliff shook his head. 'What then?'

'I just – take my turn at lookout,' said Cliff. 'And – uh – I burned a bridge.'

'The hell you did,' frowned Stretch. 'Anybody on the bridge when you set it afire? Pursuit party? A stagecoach?'

'Nobody,' said Cliff. 'I burned it – so a posse couldn't stay after Tragg's bunch. Then I caught up with 'em and said what I done for 'em and – and how I wanted to join up with 'em. And Tragg took to me right off. I think he likes me.'

'I don't,' retorted Stretch. 'But thanks for the booze and the smoke. If a posse raids this roost, maybe I'll put in a word for you. But, meantime, keep your mouth shut, hear? If any of them bastards learns one word you and me said to each other – no deal. You got that?'

'I got that,' winced Cliff.

He took the medical kit back to the cabin, returned and resumed his perch on the box in front of the tent.

And now Stretch could meditate again, in pain. The balm helped a little, the whiskey more, but the memories were as sharp, memories of the sting of the lash wielded by a man who hated him, a rogue who had decreed he should die in agony and slowly.

'Wherever you are, runt, I hope you're gettin' close,' he mused. 'If you can reach me, get rid of these ropes and put a gun in my hand, we'll likely fight our last fight. But, before we go down shootin', one of these buzzards has to get his, and I hope it's me gives it to him.'

By 2 pm, Larry was exhausted, perched on a ledge barely a foot and a half wide, his back planted against the hard surface of the mountainside, his legs dangling, his gear beside him. He had recoiled his line. When he stopped panting, he began chewing jerky and assessing his progress. No way would he look downward; nausea was exactly what he did *not* need. He had no option but to rest before resuming his risky ascent.

Twisting slightly, he raised his eyes to the heights. Not quite so far away now. No, sir. Nowhere near as far. He calculated he had climbed better than halfway up the crater's north side. And he decided he should forget – or try to – the bad moments, hand-over-hand ascents, his loop tight around an outcropping directly above, his line taut, he fretting every second of every minute, fearing his formidable weight would be too much for the joined lariats knotted to the surplus rope by which Slow Wolf had hung, awaiting the attack of the mountain lion, fearing the outcropping would give way. Three times he had been forced to use this method; parts of the mountainside were just too steep to take a chance on finding handholds, footholds.

When he stopped chewing, he allowed himself the comfort of tobacco, just one thinly-rolled quirley of Bull Durham. He studied the area still to be climbed, craning his neck. Not too steep, he observed. Maybe he would reach the top without having to lasso another outcropping, another jutting rock that might or might not be embedded firmly enough to stay in position.

His cigarette burned down, he butted it, flexed his muscles and decided he was ready for more. He reslung his Winchester and his partner's belted Colts, then the coiled rope, then rose to his feet and, with his arms spread, plotted another ascent, eyes questing for whatever he could take hold of, whatever indentations he could fit a boot into. Take your time, he warned himself. Try hustling and you could make that one big mistake – and take a fall no human nor animal could survive.

'All right,' he reflected. 'Like the beanpole always says, here we go again.'

He raised a foot, dug it in, heaved himself upward and got his leathered-gloved hands to a crack, raising himself higher. So it began, a slow, nerve-racking, muscle-aching ascent with sweat trickling into his eyes and breaking out all over his brawny torso, causing his underwear and shirt to cling and itch.

After what seemed an eternity, he heaved himself over onto flat, hard ground, crawled ten yards to the concealment of a large boulder and flopped. Well, he had made it, his head swimming, ears tingling, breathing irregular. He sprawled face-down for a long time, bone-weary and winded, thinking, 'You get no younger – nor stronger.'

When he finally caught his wind and could breathe normally, he gave himself credit, figuring he deserved it. Sure, he wasn't getting any younger; every man ages day by day. But his strength? He couldn't be weakening, slowing down. Hell, no. He was here, wasn't he? He had achieved his goal. He felt for his watch and squinted at it. Son of a gun. 4.45. Still daylight. So now he could survey the Pronto Gang's roost.

He glanced to right and left. In places, the crater rim was less than six feet wide, in other sections, ten yards or more. Edging his face out from behind the rock, he scanned the opposite rim and at once spotted the lookout. No difficult chore; the man wore a brightly patterned poncho. Checking the terrain west. As Larry could see only his back, that was obvious enough. He crawled clear of the rock to the inner edge to stare down at the camp. With profound relief, he observed the near slope was gentle. A descent would be easy, provided he didn't dislodge rubble that would betray his presence. The slant was liberally dotted with brush-clumps and boulders so, when the time came, yes, he could get down there.

Next question: was his partner still alive and, if so, where were they holding him?

He studied the outlet from the natural tunnel, the secret entrance, then the rough shelters, plank and tarpaper most of them. The one substantial-looking structure he guessed to be the boss-bandit's personal quarters. Three fires going and, of course, their smoke rose only half-way to the crater-rim before evaporating. A spring almost dead centre of the crater's floor, so no water shortage here. He counted the men he could see, seven of them. The others, he assumed, occupied tents or lean-tos. Every man well-armed – naturally.

Now he yearned for his field-glasses, craving a

closer study of the man perched on a box a short distance in front of a tent almost directly below. That one, even from this height, looked to be younger than the hard-cases hunkered about fires or currying horses in the pole corral. Emma's brother? If so, why didn't he budge?

Before thrusting his head out to stare downward, he made sure the lookout still squatted facing west. He glimpsed the tattered tent, withdrew and dropped flat again. Could the kid be sitting guard on a prisoner? He grinned inwardly. They wouldn't post a guard on a dead man. He was ready to bet his partner was in that tent, no doubt hogtied. So he was being kept alive, but for how long?

Fifteen minutes later, more activity down there, supper being cooked on the three fires. That reminded him of his own hunger. He bit off another chaw of jerky, munched and waited.

What he next saw confirmed his hunch. The man on the box rose and moved to a fire when summoned, and now he was sure the man was young – very. It had to be Emma Dane's brother who collected a heaped plate and a mug of coffee and retraced his steps to enter the shabby tent.

'You're the kid outlaw; somebody I've known most of my life's stuck in that tent,' he assured himself. 'And, soon as it's dark enough, I have to get down there.'

He warily studied the slope he would descend, memorizing patches of brush and clusters of boulders that would give him cover. Moonlight could aid him. He must move clear of soft sections, earth or pebbles that might roll – noisily – giving him away.

Returning to the big rock, he squatted, waiting for sundown, while Emma Dane and the hefty half-breed lurked in the thick growth opposite the camouflaged door.

SEVEN
Getting Close

'I know the lookout's position,' Emma said tensely. 'I saw him clearly.'

'I too,' nodded Slow Wolf. 'But he watches the ground far to the west. He does not look straight down. I believe, Emma, no searcher ever came this close, ever actually *saw* the entrance.'

'He'd have detected movement through the brush but for your ...' She was about to use the expression "Indian savvy". It didn't seem polite, applied to this erudite misfit, 'your natural skills.'

'One remembers one's boyhood tuition,' he said. 'Pater was never a success as a warrior. More foolhardy than courageous, I'd say. But, at hunting and stalking, as skilful as any of his tribesmen. There are ways, and fortunately I remember them, of penetrating heavy brush without disturbing it.'

'I couldn't have made it alone, Chief.'

'You did well, dear lady, simply by imitating my movements.'

'All that crawling and slithering ...'

'Uncomfortable, but essential.'

'We're here,' she softly. 'We've followed Larry's orders and – now comes the hard part – the worst part.'

'The waiting.' He winced, nudged five inches of jerky into his mouth and began chewing. 'A long wait, I'm afraid.'

'If I only knew how he is at this moment,' she sighed. 'He could be dead, Chief. Can't dismiss that possibility, can we? He may have climbed – terribly high – then a frayed rope or a rock giving way under him ...'

'Come, my dear, such pessimism is unworthy of you,' he chided.

'... and he'd have fallen to his death,' she fretted.

She lapsed into silence. So did he, for a minute or two. Then he confided, 'This is a new and strange experience for me. I cannot recall when last I conversed with a white woman in this way.'

'You mean as an educated gentleman,' she supposed.

'Prudence requires my assuming the typical broken English of the redman when addressing white strangers,' he said ruefully. 'Uncouth whites, poorly schooled or, in many cases, quite illiterate, can be so *sensitive*. I daren't depart from the ridiculous patter they expect of me.' He treated her to a few examples. 'Me honest Injun, no make trouble for white brothers. Fetch 'um heap good deer-meat. You trade for wampum?'

'Stop it.' He had made her smile again. '*That's* unworthy of *you*.'

'Would it seem an unpardonable liberty if I dared advise you?' he asked.

'Go ahead.' She was prone beside him, elbows propped, chin cupped in her hands. 'There are more than a few years between us, so advise by all means.'

'You are in error on two counts,' he assured her. 'One – it's unlikely Lawrence fell to his death. Were he no longer among the living, my instincts would tell me so. I would sense his demise and would mourn him. He will do what he set out to do.'

'Invade the outlaw camp and free Stretch,' she mused. 'I know he's brilliant in some ways and uncommonly lucky, but ...'

'He *and* Woodville have performed quite incredible feats,' he declared.

'So it's a mistake for me to fear for his life,' she nodded. 'You said I'm in error on two counts. What's my other mistake, Chief?'

'I hesitate,' he said uncomfortably. 'This is – so personal.'

'If you think it has to be said, say it,' she urged.

'Your other mistake, and a sad mistake it would be, so I urge you to practise restraint ...'

'Chief, get to the point.'

'It is natural for you to admire my good friend Lawrence, as I admire him. But, I beg you, follow your mind and the laws of reason – not your heart. It's a good heart, Emma. I would be sad if it were broken, and broken it would be if you lost control of your emotions.'

'So – you've guessed.'

'Instinct. Injun savvy if you wish.'

'Look, I know it's hopeless.'

'It *is* hopeless, Emma. For some of us, Lawrence, Woodville, I too and another valued cohort – his name is Beaumont – there can be no settled existence, no commitments to restrict us. We are nomads and we don't deceive ourselves, we admit to it, accept it, see ourselves for what we are. We don't despise the opposite sex, but in fairness we have to avoid emotional involvement. Marriage rarely cures the wanderlust. We who are born to roam will simply continue to roam.' Having delivered that warning, the half-Sioux apologized. 'If my words offend, I'll never forgive myself.'

She shook her head and said resignedly, 'Never beg pardon for being truthful, Chief. It *is* true, everything you've said. I knew before I met him – and meeting him was something I never anticipated – the kind of man Larry is. And I doubt he ever tried to impress a woman. The trouble is ...' she showed Slow Wolf a sad smile, 'he doesn't know just how impressive he *is*. Simply by being himself, big, resolute, protective and dependable, he can arouse all kinds of feelings, yearnings, in all kinds of women.'

'He has always been a strong personality,' said Slow Wolf. 'Woodville tends to be gauche. Yes, quite guileless, so much so that his adversaries have too often underestimated him. They're such opposites, my Texas friends.'

'But Stretch can be just as tough when needs be,' she said.

'Indeed yes,' he said. 'Together, fighting side by side, they are a quite fearsome duo.'

'I pray Stretch is still alive,' she murmured. 'But, even if Larry can reach him, even if he's still strong enough to fight, they'll be only two against so many. We could help, Chief, but only if we can get past that door – and who'd open it for us?'

'Under cover of darkness, Lawrence perhaps,' he said. 'When he reaches the northern heights of the crater, the descent into the hideout may be easier, and it's not entirely impossible he could make his way to the tunnel unseen.'

'So ...' She nodded slowly. 'We can only cling to that hope.'

After sundown, the guard on the crater rim was relieved. Larry waited, studying the activity around the camp. Raucous laughter reached him, indicating the Pronto Gang was in festive mood. He saw Cliff Dane approach one of the cookfires and assumed Stretch was to be fed again.

That assumption both pleased and disquieted him. Knowing his partner's appetite so well, it was some relief to know he was being kept fed regularly. But why? Were there humane hard-cases in this wolf-pack? It didn't seem likely. What did seem likely was that, for their own reasons, they were keeping Stretch alive – but what *were* their reasons?

'Maybe *he* knows,' he reflected. 'I'll have to remember to ask him when I get to him.'

When, not if. He doggedly rejected all thoughts of failing to reach his partner. Hell, he hadn't climbed that damn mountainside, risked his neck, just for the thrill of it.

Cliff loaded two plates, remarking to Elmo Stark, 'I can feed him and eat at the same time.'

'That's right, Kid,' grinned Stark. 'Keep his belly full, keep him strong. That's how Jethro wants him. He'll have a hearty breakfast too. And then, after *he* eats, he'll work on Emerson some more.'

Cliff managed an answering grin and succeeded in sounding eager as he asked, 'What's it to be next time?'

'Jethro aims to burn him some,' chuckled Stark. 'Said he'll likely blind the bastard. But that won't be the end of it for Emerson. The most fun Jethro's had in a long time is plannin' how slow he's gonna finish that hero off.'

Coldly patient now, Stretch listened to the approaching footsteps. Cliff toted the plates into the tent, set them down and hunkered beside him.

'I can't see to eat,' he complained.

'You don't have to,' muttered Cliff. 'I can see your mouth.'

He fed the prisoner several mouthfuls, ate some of his own food and brooded.

'Sounds like every son's happy,' Stretch remarked, cocking an ear. 'Big celebration tonight?'

'Yeah, sure,' grunted Cliff. 'You ready for more?'

'Always,' nodded Stretch. 'Keep that chow comin', boy.' A few moments later, he casually enquired, 'Been doin' some thinkin'?'

'You know I didn't relish what I saw,' mumbled Cliff. 'Him layin' into you with that whip.'

'I didn't relish the feel of it,' shrugged Stretch. 'You only had to watch. I had to take it.' He downed another mouthful. 'But that ain't enough to satisfy Tragg, huh? He got somethin' else in store for me?'

'I dunno,' said Cliff.

'My partner can tell when a man's lyin' most times,' said Stretch. 'I'm pretty smart at that myself. C'mon, Reno, you've heard somethin' – so you might's well tell me.'

Cliff gagged on a half-chewed mouthful, coughed, swallowed and grimaced.

'It's better I don't tell you.'

'Do it,' Stretch quietly ordered.

'Stark says …' faltered Cliff, 'he says Tragg aims to – burn your eyes out.'

It stunned him that the tall captive took that as calmly as if he'd been told Tragg intended giving him a haircut. His only comment was, 'I hope you still admire your boss – and the other scum you've joined up with.'

'You know I can't help you,' sighed Cliff.

'Better think twice about that,' advised Stretch. 'What they said about my partner, don't count on it. No way could they hold him in that Kingsville calaboose. There was a witness, the local sawbones, and five'll get you ten he straightened the sheriff out. Just 'tween you and me, kid, Larry's been headed thisaway since a little while after Werris's bunch took me out of Kingsville. I'd say a day at most.'

'He couldn't …' began Cliff.

'Couldn't get closer'n all them posses?' challenged Stretch. 'Don't bet your ass on it. He can follow sign smart as any Injun. Who the hell d'you think taught him and me trail-savvy? Comanches, boy.'

'I don't reckon he could find the way in here,' frowned Cliff. 'And, even if he did …'

'Right,' nodded Stretch. 'He couldn't get past that door – unless. And you know what comes after unless. Somebody, some smart young'un hankerin' to save his own butt, is gonna have to lift that iron bar and open up for him.'

'They'd kill me for that,' protested Cliff.

'They don't have to see you do it,' countered Stretch. 'And he could show up any time. Tonight even.'

'It ain't dark enough,' fretted Cliff. 'Too much

moonlight.'

'Could be done,' insisted Stretch. 'You'd have to pick your time.'

'Even if he got in, he couldn't lick the whole outfit all by himself.' Cliff shook his head worriedly. 'Hell. He'd be one against ...'

'Thirteen – or just a dozen?' prodded Stretch. 'Might be gettin' near time for you to decide whichaway you're gonna jump, young feller. You're with these sonsabitches – or us.'

'You mean you and Valentine?' said Cliff. 'Nothin' *you* could do.'

'Plenty I can do when the time comes,' Stretch said gently. 'If you can work up the nerve to loosen my ropes and get me a shootin' iron. That'd make three of us.'

'Oh, hell,' groaned Cliff.

'Your chance'd be as good as ours,' Stretch assured him. 'From good cover, you could do your share. If you're any use with that pistol, and if you can grab yourself a rifle. Any grub left?' Cliff resumed feeding him. Then, when the plate was empty, he asked, 'You gonna fetch me some coffee now?'

'Back in a minute,' said Cliff.

Larry had begun his descent, but was taking his time, going to pains to escape detection. He slid into the concealment of a brush-clump a quarter way down the inside slope when he saw the young man quit the flimsy tent and carry the empty plates to a cookfire.

As Cliff filled two cups from the coffee-pot, one of the other men with Stark asked, 'You tell Emerson he'll be a blind man by noon tomorrow?'

It struck Cliff Dane that he was becoming quite

an actor, an expert in fact. He was able to laugh sardonically.

'I sure did,' he replied. 'And – hey – if you could've seen the look on his dumb face. Boy, is he scared!'

'Should've happened to Emerson a long time back, ten, fifteen years, him and Valentine both,' said Stark. 'They've been playin' hero far too long.'

'Damn right,' agreed Cliff.

Larry watched him return to the tent with the coffee, marked the positions of all the men he could see. None glancing to this slope. He moved again, easing himself down toward a man-sized boulder. This would take time, he warned himself. The most he could hope for was that he'd be on flat ground directly behind Stretch's canvas prison before the sun rose.

Cliff held a cup to Stretch's mouth. He gulped a few mouthfuls and again drew his jailer into conversation.

'You got folks, Reno?'

'I'm an orphan,' said Cliff.

'Me and Larry too,' drawled Stretch. 'Listen, it ain't gonna make no difference, so you might's well tell me. You got no kin at all?'

'Just a sister. Used to try bossin' me around.'

'For your own good, I bet. What's your real name?'

'None of your business.'

'Have it your way. Well? You been thinkin'?'

'I dunno what to do.'

'The hell you don't. I told you plain enough.'

'And I – damn it – I need more time for thinkin'.'

'Ain't the best coffee I ever had, but I could use all of it.'

As Cliff slowly tipped the tin cup, Stretch drained it. Grudgingly, Cliff observed, 'You don't act scared.'

'Frettin' never helped a man,' shrugged Stretch. 'What matters is what a man *does*.'

'Seems to me you take a lot for granted, big feller,' said Cliff. 'Anything could've happened to your partner, even if he was turned loose. I mean 'tween Kingsville and here. Suppose for instance he *was* tailin' you and Werris and the others ...'

'They'd never know it,' Stretch said with a hard grin. 'Next to me, he's the smartest bird-dogger ever rid out of Texas.'

'All right, but what about the nights?' challenged Cliff. 'By now, he could be dead of pneumonia because he never dared show light, fix a fire to save himself from freezin'.'

'Some hombres're too blame hotheaded to freeze,' said Stretch. 'He's feelin' plenty mad and, believe me, when my ol' buddy gets mad, he gets hot all over, hot enough to melt a snowdrift.'

'How can you be sure he didn't get slowed down anyway?' persisted Cliff. 'Why couldn't his horse go lame? Or what if, while he was hidin', he got bit by a rattler? I don't see how you can count on ...'

'We've been countin' on each other the longest time, kid,' Stretch said wistfully. 'He gets in a fix, I'm there to help him out. I'm in trouble, he settles it for me. We've saved each other's hides oftener'n we can keep tally. Me countin' on Larry is just somethin' comes natural. Like breathin'.'

'I can't keep lingerin' in here with you,' said Cliff, rising abruptly. 'Somebody's liable to get leery.'

'So go plant your butt on that doggone box,'

urged Stretch. 'And keep ponderin' what you're gonna do when the chips're down.'

Till midnight, Larry squatted behind the boulder. Too much activity down below, Pronto men moving around. They kept feeding the fires, though the high country chill hadn't invaded the hideout. He supposed, with the area ringed by so much rock, a natural crater, the wind's full force was buffered.

He heard shouts and edged his head around to put one eye on the sturdiest of the shacks. More than one lamp lit that building. The tall man emerging from it, laughing stridently and waving a bottle, was clearly silhouetted. Jethro Tragg was in a mood for company, needing an audience; this was his night to brag. The lookout was relieved and most of the other men converged on Tragg's shack, all their attention focused on him. He took advantage of this diversion, climbed down to a lower vantage-point and, by the glow of the fires and the light of the moon, got his bearings.

By working his way to an outcropping of brush, he would be almost directly above and behind the tent housing his partner. Still a long descent but, if his luck held, he could be joining Stretch before dawn.

Now was the time for another move. He made it to the brush and, as he flopped again, stifled a yawn. A reminder, he grudgingly acknowledged. He was only human. Unless he allowed himself a couple of hours of sleep, he would be in poor shape for whatever lay ahead.

And so, screened by the outcropping, he lay on his back and closed his eyes.

The first sun-rays brought him back to

awareness. He sat up, listening intently. All was quiet. A downward glance was all it took to convince him nobody else was stirring. The young man on the box fronting the tent sat with head bowed, dozing. In the shacks and other tents, the desperadoes were sleeping off last night's jag; the party must have ended late. He stared up to the opposite side in time to see the lookout rise, stretch and glance down to the crater floor. When the man resumed his perch, turning his back again, Larry broke cover and began a faster descent.

Level ground at last, about seven yards of it between the base of the slope and the back of the tattered and torn shelter. He crept to it, lifted rotted canvas and peered inside. Stretch promptly rolled over and softly remarked, 'What kept you, runt?'

Eyes gleaming, jaw tightening, Larry crawled in, let the canvas fall behind him and surveyed his partner, huddled with his torn shirt and the top half of his underwear bunched about his loins, his back lacerated, wrists and ankles bound, face bruised and showing dry blood – also showing the familiar grin. For a tense moment, he was incapable of speech, so all-consuming was his fury. So Stretch drawled another remark.

'Took your sweet time gettin' to me.' He added a warning as Larry made to speak. 'Talk soft.'

'So how the hell d'you think I made it?' mumbled Larry, moving to him.

'Outside wall,' guessed Stretch.

'Think that was easy?' grouched Larry, ridding himself of coiled rope, slung Winchester and his partner's belted .45s. 'It was straight up most of the way. I could've fallen and broke my neck – and every bone in my body.' He cursed as he studied the weals. 'Sonsabitches! What they've done to you ...!'

'It's kind of convenient you gettin' here now,' Stretch told him. 'Yesterday, their boss-man, a two-legged skunk name of Jethro Tragg, used a whip on me – like you can see. Today, he plans on blindin' me.' As Larry produced his jack-knife, he shook his head. 'Nope. Don't cut these ropes. Better you loose the knots so I can pull free when I need to. I still ain't sure about the kid out front. Maybe he'll side us, maybe he won't.'

While working on the wrist-ropes, Larry asked, 'He tell you his name?'

'Just calls himself the Reno Kid,' said Stretch.

'Reno Kid my ass,' scowled Larry. 'Cliff Dane's his name. A sassy tearaway with a dumb hankerin' for outlawry. His sister joined up with me. Her and Slow Wolf're hid in the brush, and you can guess where.'

'Where'd you find our ol' buddy the Chief?'

'On our way here.'

'You mean *healthy*? Hell, runt, the bastards that brought me here, they roughed him up and left him danglin' – bait for a big cat. You found him before ...'

'Let me put it this way. If we'd rounded that bend a minute later'n we did, you and me wouldn't have a half-Sioux compadre no more.'

In muttered undertones, they did some catching up while Stretch rubbed at his chafed wrists and tried his feet. He recounted all that had befallen him since he succumbed to whatever had been used to spike his whiskey. Larry, helping him fit his torso into the remains of his upper garments, offered a terse summary of his own movements since beginning his search; his meeting with Emma Dane, Slow Wolf's discovery of the camouflaged log door and his own arduous ascent of the crater's north wall.

Stretch then remembered the buried bottle. They each took a stiff swig. Flexing and unflexing his hands, caressing his wrists, the taller Texan stared longingly at his sidearms.

'Want to try heftin' 'em before I rope you again?' Larry asked softly.

'Hands feel fine – for a wonder,' muttered Stretch. 'But I guess I better.'

Larry proffered the weapons. Stretch slid them from their holsters, hefted them, twirled them by their trigger-guards and nodded grimly.

'Uh-huh,' grunted Larry. 'This won't be your day for gettin' your eyes burned out.'

Stretch returned his Colts to their holsters and squatted, hands behind his back. Larry ran the ropes around wrists and ankles, but loosely, not knotting them, though it would not seem so to the youth assigned to guard him. The other rope, Larry's Winchester and Stretch's sidearms were placed by Larry to the left of the forward flap.

'How're we gonna get this done?' asked Stretch. 'There's thirteen of 'em, runt, not countin' the kid.'

'We'll be four after Emma and the Chief stake out the inside of the tunnel,' said Larry.

'Only one way they can get in,' frowned Stretch. 'That door'll only open from this side.'

'That'll be the kid's chore,' said Larry. 'But he don't know it yet.' He moved to the right of the flap and dropped hand to holster. 'Call to him, but not too loud, just so long as you get him in here. You're thirsty. Better still, you're hungry.'

'Meanin' *you're* hungry,' guessed Stretch.

'You know it,' winced Larry.

Stretch resumed his prone position and called to his guard.

'Hey, Reno, can you hear me out there? I could sure use some more grub.'

Peering through a rent in the canvas, Larry saw Cliff Dane bestir himself. Stiff-legged and yawning, he trudged to the nearest fire, found a plate and ladled sustenance from a cookpot. He was yawning when he moved to the tent. Just inside the entrance, he froze. The muzzle of Larry's Colt prodded his left ear – through which he heard the gut-churning sound of the hammer being thumbed back.

'One yelp, Cliffy boy, and you're grave-bait,' Larry softly warned.

'And, for Pete's sake, don't spook and drop that chow,' pleaded Stretch. 'My partner's hungry. If that plate hits the dirt, he'll kick your ass and *then* blow your brains out.'

'Lord Almighty!' breathed Cliff.

'Nope, Larry Valentine,' corrected Stretch.

'Move in, set the plate down, keep your paw far clear of your holster,' ordered Larry.

Cliff obeyed. Larry edged closer to the flap to keep the camp under observation.

'Pick it up again, Cliff,' urged Stretch. 'Give it to my ol' buddy. Right now, he's hungrier'n me.'

Larry holstered his six-gun, accepted the plate and began eating, still scanning the area outside, while Cliff gawked at him.

'How – how'd *he* get here?'

'Climbed the north wall,' drawled Stretch.

'Nobody could do that!' protested Cliff.

'Wasn't nobody that did it,' Stretch patiently explained. 'It was *somebody*, meanin' Larry.'

'It can't be done.' Cliff was still in shock.

'D'you see him or don't you?' grinned Stretch.

'And – he knows my name,' fretted Cliff.

'Damn fool kid like you don't deserve such a sister,' Larry mumbled while munching. 'Emma was huntin' you and I was taggin' Stretch and the polecats that kidnapped him. We met up. She's waitin' yonder of that trick door with a friend of ours.'

'Emma – out there?' The young man shook his head and sighed heavily. 'Oh, hell. I sure messed up.'

'We'll have a couple extra guns backin' us after you let 'em in,' said Larry. 'That's what you're gonna do, kid, so they can stake out this end of the tunnel.'

'I dunno how long Tragg'll wait for ...'

'When he gets impatient, we'll show ourselves. That's when the showdown'll start.'

'But you'll be outnumbered!'

'And they'll be surprised,' declared Larry.

'*Real* surprised, Cliff,' Stretch said grimly. 'That's our ace in the hole.'

Cliff looked at him, then at Larry.

'I guess – uh – you want me to cut him loose,' he said. Larry eyed him scathingly. He winced and shrugged. 'No, I guess you already did that.'

'Take this.' Larry handed him the empty plate. 'Take it back to the fire, then come plant your butt on that box again – and wait.'

'Try not to look spooked, sonny,' advised

Stretch. 'Don't tip our hand. Leave *that* to *us*. Just do like Larry told you.'

'If you're with us,' said Larry. 'And you'd *better* be.'

'I'm with you,' nodded Cliff. 'Honest, I swear I never figured Emma'd try to find me. If I'd believed …'

'You ought to get to know your sister,' muttered Larry. 'It'd be good for your health. Stand by her, heed her, and you could have some kind of future. No future for outlaws, boy. Any fool can figure that for himself.'

'Maybe …' Cliff, stung by Larry's words, felt a sudden urge to redeem himself. 'Maybe I could reach the tunnel – and the door – before they come alive.'

Larry glanced out front again.

'All right, give it a try, but stay cool,' he cautioned. 'Act casual.'

Stretch rid himself of his ropes, rose and joined his partner to watch Cliff Dane saunter unhurriedly to the fire, drop the plate, then saunter on, making for the outlet of the tunnel.

'There'll be a lookout on the west wall, runt.'

'I know,' said Larry. 'Red poncho. It'll take a rifle-slug to score on him from down here. I won't be forgettin' him.'

'What's she like, the kid's sister?' asked Stretch.

'Older'n him and a hundred percent smarter,' said Larry. 'Rigged like a man, thinks like a man, packs a six-gun and a Winchester and – this you can believe – she's a sure shot.'

'The Chief gonna be okay?'

'Makes like he's stiff-scared, but you know him. He'll do his share. I loaned him your rifle. They stole his.' Larry's mouth set in a hard line. 'Took his Winchester, beat up on him, left him hangin' for that crazy cougar to butcher. Some fine bunch of hero-bandidos, this Pronto bunch.'

'Mean and lowdown, runt,' muttered Stretch. 'We've gone up against some bad'uns, but I'm tellin' you they're the worst.'

'Think you have to convince me?' challenged Larry. 'I've seen what Tragg did to your back. It must be givin' you hell.'

'Smarts some,' frowned Stretch. 'But a little pain ain't gonna slow me down. They've been feedin' me regular, so I still got my strength.' He paced the small area in which he'd been confined, relishing the sensation of freedom of movement. 'How's the kid doin'?'

'Gettin' closer,' Larry reported. 'Uh-huh. Now he's snuck into the tunnel.' He changed position slightly to peer up to the heights, but could not glimpse the lookout from here. A few more moments and he was studying the tunnel exit again. 'He's comin' out now. Guess he had time to lift the bar and open the door a mite. The Chief won't miss that.'

'Got eyes like a wolf, our lard-bellied buddy,' grinned Stretch. 'A slow wolf, but he don't miss nothin'.'

'Kid's comin' back,' said Larry. 'Makin' for where he's supposed to squat.' He cocked an ear. 'And now I hear voices. Sounds like the whole bunch's comin' alive.'

'Some of 'em gonna be hung over good,' opined Stretch. 'That'll give us an edge.'

Men emerged from shelters, strapping on sidearms, hefting rifles, making for the fires to cook breakfast. Soon, vengeance-hungry Tragg would crave sadistic action. And the trouble-shooters would be ready.

EIGHT

Give No Quarter

From where they waited in the brush, Slow Wolf and the woman heard the sounds from beyond the camouflaged entrance, faint at first, then the thud of the discarded bar. While they watched, the overgrown door swung inward a few inches. Emma caught a fleeting glimpse of her brother's face and her heart leapt, but she resisted the urge to call his name. The face disappeared.

'It was Cliff!' she whispered.

The half-breed nodded, edged forward a few feet and cautiously raised his head to scan the heights.

'If I cannot see the lookout, we can safely assume we are as invisible to him,' he muttered.

'You know what this means,' she said.

'All too well, Emma,' he winced. 'All too well.'

'Our time has come,' she declared. 'Ready, Chief?'

'Ready,' he sighed. 'I won't say willing. But, yes, ready.'

They broke cover, hurried across to the door and leaned against it. With the opening now two feet wide, they could see along the natural tunnel to its outlet and beyond.

'That's where we stake out,' she reminded him as they moved in. 'The other end – the inside end.'

'As unobtrusively as possible,' he pleaded.

He closed the entrance and followed Emma to within a few feet of the outlet. There, they bellied down and, side by side, crawled forward for their first appraisal of the outlaw camp.

Men were astir, some of them familiar to the pudgy redman; he shuddered, plagued by harrowing memories of his dangling helpless, awaiting the attack of a mountain lion crazed with pain. Emma scanned the scene from ground level and sighted her brother again.

'Over to the other side,' she whispered. 'Sitting on a box in front of the shabbiest tent in the place. You see him?'

'So young,' Slow Wolf sadly observed. 'How tragic the waywardness of the young ...'

'It *was* him, Chief. He opened up for us, and that can only mean Larry's here. Somehow, he got to Cliff, won him over. Or, more likely, he bullied and threatened him into co-operating with us.'

'I expect Lawrence only needed to mention your name.'

'Our orders are clear. We have to wait till ...'

'Yes, till the first shots are fired. Or – until some rogue moves in our direction. If we are discovered, my dear Emma, we'll have no option but to take the initiative.'

'I'm sure Larry realizes that.'

They hugged the ground, nobody glancing their way. Werris was carrying two laden platters and a coffee-pot to the Tragg cabin. The other men were eating, taking their time about it.

Not for the first time in their hectic career, the Texans played the waiting game, concealed in the old tent, watching the opposition, awaiting the inevitable. The next move, as far as they were concerned, was up to the leader of this pack of homicidal predators.

Calmly, Stretch warned his partner, 'Your first kill has to be the hombre sittin' lookout. You got no choice, runt. From up there, he'd get a clear bead on us soon as we show ourselves.'

'I'm keepin' him in mind,' Larry assured him.

'No matter how many of 'em're in front of us, I figure I can spook 'em, start a scatter, give you time to take your best shot,' said Stretch.

'After that, we'll be busy a while,' predicted Larry. He was as calm as Stretch, his nerves rock-steady; he might have been pondering a simple chore, such as how best to flush a half-dozen strays out of a clump of chaparral. 'Mighty useful, the kid openin' up for Emma and the Chief. When the shootin' starts, they'll buy in and these coyotes'll be caught in our crossfire.'

'Sounds good to me,' Stretch said bitterly. 'I owe these sidewinders, runt.'

'*We* owe 'em,' insisted Larry. 'The Chief too. They ain't my idea of a merciful bunch, so how much mercy do they rate?'

'Tragg better not hope for any from me,' declared Stretch.

Some forty-five minutes passed with no member of the gang venturing close to the outlet. At a shouted command from inside the main cabin, men traded grins and hustled to fetch wood and build up the fire closest the spring. Stretch identified the voice for Larry's benefit. Tragg.

Another five minutes and the tall and hairy outlaw-boss was emerging from his cabin tagged by a grinning Sid Werris. Tragg's loins were girded by his double-holstered gunbelt; he seemed in high spirits despite last night's celebration.

'Elmo and Farley!' he bellowed. 'You make ready to rope that bastard Texan to them uprights again. Then I'll get me a firebrand and have me some more pleasure.' He waved to Cliff. 'On your feet, Kid! Drag him outa there!'

'Yeah, sure,' grinned Cliff, rising.

He got up, turned and made for the tent. When he entered, all Larry said was, 'You know what to do – so do it.'

Cliff moved to the rear, dropped to his knees, raised the tattered canvas and crawled away. Stretch donned his Stetson. He and Larry traded glances.

'Go on,' invited Larry, levering a shell into his Winchester's breech. 'Say it like you always do.'

'Here we go again,' Stretch remarked with relish.

They stood and waited, Larry with his rifle at the ready, Stretch with his long arms hanging loose, fingers brushing the butts of his tied-down Colts. For him, it was one of those times, a time to give thanks that, with handguns, he was ambidexterous.

The men outside, bunched some thirty-five feet from the box on which Cliff had squatted, grinned in anticipation. Then Tragg became impatient.

'Get a hustle on, Kid!' he chided. 'What're you waitin' for?'

'I'd reckon now,' suggested Larry.

'Yup,' agreed Stretch. 'Now's as good a time as any.'

With that, Larry swept the flap aside with the muzzle of his Winchester and they strode out to confront the Pronto Gang and were stared at by men frozen in shock, all but two, the first to rally, the first to drop hands to holsters, and to die.

Stretch's matched .45s were out and roaring and Larry crouching, drawing a bead on the red-ponchoed sentry now taking aim. He squeezed trigger, saw the lookout reel, drop his weapon and fall to the slope to roll to the crater floor. The two mortally wounded by Stretch lurched against their cohorts and the morning air was blasted by a din of gunfire. The outlaws were scattering, the Texans dodging and weaving and, from the tunnel outlet, Emma and Slow Wolf cutting loose, challenging the opposition with well-aimed .44.40 slugs. Two more were down, writhing in the dust.

For the moment, the trouble-shooters had to concentrate on just staying alive. Larry had emptied his holster and ducked and not a second too soon. He scored on the man who triggered the bullet cutting through space filled by his torso an instant before. Stretch was sidestepping, still shooting fast, the horses in the corral neighing shrilly and Tragg, Werris, Stark and Murquette beelining for the main cabin, snapping shots over their shoulders. They were inside the cabin before Stretch thought to probe the rising dust for familiar faces.

The nearest cover was the built-up fire. With Stretch at his heels, Larry headed in that direction. Somewhere to his right, he heard six-guns roaring and glimpsed two running men shooting at other targets; the other intruders, Emma and Slow Wolf, had been spotted. From inside the tunnel, Winchesters barked again and the two loosed yells and pitched to the dust.

'Stay right where you are!' Larry called to Emma, as he and Stretch put the fire between them and Tragg's cabin.

'I think we've accounted for . . .!' she began.

'I know it!' he roared. 'Eight down – four to go!'

'Where the hell's the kid?' wondered Stretch, while they ejected spent shells and reloaded.

'Behind cover and keepin' his head down – if his head's got a brain in it,' growled Larry.

A rifle barked from a window of the cabin. The slug ploughed into the fire, spattering them with ash and sparks. Stretch grimaced indignantly and was moved to remark, 'You know – uh – this ain't the best cover we ever hid behind of.'

'I noticed,' nodded Larry. 'You complainin'?'

'Just remarkin',' said Stretch.

'Remark all you want,' invited Larry. 'You're right anyway.'

Their Colts were reloaded when the harsh voice reached them, ragged, strident. Tragg was irate.

'Emerson – you hear me, Emerson? You're gonna be a dead man real soon! For what you did to Ruben, I ain't lettin' you outa here alive!'

Larry promptly retorted, 'This is Valentine! If you and them other three polecats crave to stay alive, come on out of there gunless and with your paws high!'

'I call that big talk!' jeered Murquette. 'From a damn fool pinned behind of a fire!'

From the cabin window, rifles barked again. The Texans bowed their heads, their hats their only shield against the rising sparks and dislodged blazing faggots.

'The hell with this,' scowled Larry, holstering his Colt. 'It could last for as long as their ammunition holds out – and they probably got plenty in that shack.'

He drew a two-foot long piece of wood from the fire. Stretch nodded approvingly.

'If you can land a couple on that plank roof, we'll smoke 'em out.'

'Get ready to give me coverin' fire,' urged Larry. 'You better trigger at the window and the doorway.'

'Bueno,' grunted Stretch. 'Ready as I'll ever be. Say when.'

'When!' breathed Larry.

They rose together, he with his right arm drawn back, taking aim while Stretch's booming Colts provided the necessary distraction. He threw and they ducked and the firebrand soared in an arc and dropped to the plank roof. The dry timber at once ignited.

'Again,' Stretch begged with a harsh grin.

The second time, a rifle-slug came so close that its hot wind fanned Larry's right ear, but he made another accurate throw. They repeated the process a few moments later, then dropped, watching, awaiting developments. Stretch grouched he was short on shells, tugged some from his partner's belt and reloaded.

Now the roof was ablaze, one of its planks rising, curling, another sagging, coming free and pitching inside the building. There was a sudden flare; the walls began burning.

'Hell!' gasped Stretch.

'They must've stored coal-oil in there,' said Larry. He bellowed at the top of his voice. 'Last chance! Come on out – but don't come shootin'!'

While he watched the blazing shack, his

partner's eyes strayed; Stretch was wondering about Cliff Dane, scanning the area east and south.

He thought he detected movement over by a wood-heap. And then he was sure, because Cliff rose into view, face contorted in agony, his right arm bloody from shoulder to wrist. Emma's brother took a few stumbling steps before the taller Texan yelled urgently, 'Stay down, kid! Just flop, damn it!'

He could have saved his breath. Cliff lacked the strength to stay on his feet; he collapsed.

'Here they come,' Larry grimly announced.

Stretch rose with him and they stepped clear of the fire, Colts cocked and ready. The four dashed out the doorway of the burning cabin followed by clouds of smoke. They toted sacks and saddlebags, but one-handed. Larry's demand had been ignored. They each gripped six-guns and those weapons were roaring, challenging the trouble-shooters, who promptly crouched and returned fire.

Larry cursed as a slug burned his left side four inches below his armpit. He lurched, but with his Colt booming, his aim true. He scored on Stark, then Werris, while Stretch relived his memories of the sting of a whiplash, bared his teeth and cut loose at Tragg and Murquette, his .45s thundering mercilessly. And, through the mist of cordite fumes and smoke from the burning cabin, he saw Murquette shudder and sag, saw Tragg, his eyes still wild with hate, lurch drunkenly with his chest a mass of red, his gun slipping from a suddenly nerveless hand. Then Tragg was down and unmoving, as dead as Werris, Stark, Murquette and all the others.

For a long moment, the tall men stood quiet,

panting. Then Larry turned and called to Slow Wolf.

'Chief?'

'A minor wound,' came Slow Wolf's reply. 'And it pleases me to assure you …'

'Emma's okay?'

'Completely unharmed.'

'Bueno. So you and me better start checkin'.'

At Larry's insistence, Stretch moved to a patch of shade to rest. Emma bounded out of the tunnel and, while Larry and Slow Wolf moved about the crater floor, inspecting every fallen man for signs of life, hurried toward Stretch.

'Cliff …?'

'Over there,' said Stretch, pointing.

Their tally finished, Larry and the redman traded sober stares. No survivors. Tragg, Werris, Stark, Murquette, Cross, Aberlain, Big Red Huber, the five who had returned with Tragg – all dead. The Pronto Gang had been wiped out.

'Your shirt – I see a tear …' Slow Wolf began solicitously.

'Never mind about me,' said Larry. 'I only got bullet-burned. Your right leg's bloody.'

'A superfluous wound.' Slow Wolf decided to be stoic. 'I am more concerned for poor Woodville. He looks to be in a somewhat reduced condition.'

Emma had reached her unconscious brother and was begging for help.

'His arm, Larry!'

'I'll take a look at him, Chief,' said Larry. 'Best you tend yourself.'

'I will return presently,' frowned Slow Wolf. 'There are certain natural medications I must gather, certain herbs.'

'Sure,' nodded Larry. 'Injun medicine.'

While Slow Wolf hurried to the tunnel to re-open the entrance, Larry moved across to where Emma knelt by her brother. She had torn the bloody sleeve away to reveal a deep gash in the right upper arm. Also, she had extricated the pistol from Cliff's hand and returned it to its holster.

'Two spent shells in the cylinder,' she reported.

'So he got off a couple shots before one of 'em downed him,' said Larry. 'And this you can believe, Emma. He wasn't shootin' at Stretch or me.'

'Can I now call him a reformed outlaw?' she asked.

'Hell, he never did get to be a real badman,' he said impatiently.

When Slow Wolf returned to them, his leg no longer bled. He had taken time to patch his own wound and was leading the horses. Larry at once called on him to stem Cliff's bleeding and, for some time thereafter, the redman played medicine-man, plying the skills taught him by his full-blood sire. At a fire, he heated water into which he scattered pieces of foliage, herbs, berries he had collected.

Emma's anxiety was eased when her brother's arm ceased to bleed. Slow Wolf applied a poultice, secured it with a clean bandanna and mumbled assurances. Her brother was young. The gash would heal fast and, soon enough, the patient would compensate for loss of blood.

Larry took a bottle from his saddlebag, pulled the cork and held the neck to Cliff's mouth, letting a little whiskey trickle in. As he gagged on it, his sister raised him to a sitting position. He coughed, groaned and opened his eyes.

'Oh, hell, Sis …'

'Be quiet,' she ordered.

'She's – mad at me,' he mumbled to Larry.

'Why *wouldn't* she be?' growled Larry. 'When I think of the bad time you gave her – and her riskin' her life to find you – well – be thankful you're hurt, kid. I never beat up on a wounded man.'

The ugly, crackling sound distracted them. Flame darted skyward from what had been Tragg's private quarters and the gang's storehouse. Stretch trudged across to join them and remark, 'We're never gonna know what was stashed in there, but it sure burns fierce.'

Flame and dancing sparks had ignited brush along the west slope. For the first time, smoke would be visible above the crater rim.

Larry hadn't thought to introduce his partner to Emma. It didn't seem to matter now, for she was talking to Stretch as though he were an old friend, questioning him about his ordeal. To his embarrassment, Slow Wolf insisted on removing his torn and ragged upper garments to inspect the damage wrought by the whip. Sighting those marks, Emma swore like a veteran cattleman and glared at the sprawled bodies.

'What d'you think, Chief?' asked Larry.

'There appears to be no infection,' frowned Slow Wolf. 'But, as they say, an ounce of prevention …' He got to his feet. 'There are other ingredients I must find. I'll be easier of mind after I've swabbed those weals. And, if Woodville has any spare clothing …'

Stretch glanced to the pack-animal, noted Larry had brought his gear along and said gratefully, 'Got a clean shirt.'

'Stay as you are,' urged Slow Wolf. 'You should not re-don those torn garments. They're filthy.'

After the half-breed left them, Larry observed Cliff was well and truly conscious. He and Emma traded stares.

'This mightn't sound right to you,' he muttered. 'All them dead bandidos layin' around – mightn't seem the time for it – but give me one good reason we oughtn't eat.'

'I'm famished,' she declared. 'The condition he's in, Cliff needs all the nourishment he can hold down, and you and Stretch must have raging appetites. No, I'm not squeamish. We have to eat, and as soon as possible.' As she rose, she added, 'We have a long journey ahead of us when we leave this place.'

While Slow Wolf swabbed Stretch's back with yet another of his own remedies, Larry wrestled with a thought, but kept it to himself. Could they ride out of here leaving so many dead unburied? If he decided his partner's abductors, his torturers, deserved burial, he would have one hell of a long and wearying chore. No way would he permit Stretch to help, nor Slow Wolf, who still limped. Cliff Dane, weakened by loss of blood and with only one good arm, couldn't participate in such a task and, even if she were willing, he would on principle reject any offer of help from Emma.

He raised his eyes. A big piece of the west slope was afire. And smoking, the smoke wafting high, as high as the crater rim. This, he reflected, would be the best of all times for a posse to be searching the Sierra Solitario. He decided to do some climbing again, this time with only his field-glasses slung from a shoulder. But not right away. Appetizing aromas reached to him from the fire at which Emma busied herself. The hell with it. If he had to again exert himself, it could wait till he had downed a hearty meal.

While the food cooked, Slow Wolf kept himself occupied. He found the Winchester stolen from him by the men who had left him to a wounded cougar's mercy and also investigated the sacks and saddlebags carried from the burning cabin by the last four to die.

'Plenty wampum, huh?' drawled Stretch. He felt better for the redman's ministrations and the feel of a clean shirt. 'Well, they bragged of lootin' many a bank, many a stagecoach.'

'What's to become of it?' wondered Slow Wolf.

'I guess we find the nearest town, runt,' Stretch suggested. 'Turn it over to the law?'

'I guess,' agreed Larry. 'But I hope there's a town closer'n Kingsville. When I remember Appleby, that bonehead sheriff, I get this hankerin' to kick his butt all the way along the main street. If I hadn't been stuck in that damn jail, none of this would've happened to you.'

Strong coffee spiked with whiskey gave Cliff a boost, as did the food dished up to him by his sister. Slow Wolf and the Texans accounted for their share and noted with approval that the cook had not exaggerated; she ate with gusto. Near the end of that much-needed meal, Cliff made his statement, eyeing Larry steadily.

'You got a right to turn me in. I was part of this outfit.'

'Was it you set fire to the bridge at Legget's Gorge?' demanded Emma. 'So Sheriff Reardon's posse couldn't pursue ...?'

'I did that,' sighed Cliff.

'You did a lot of damn fool things, boy,' chided Larry.

'But he was smart when it mattered most,' Stretch pointed out. 'By the time you told him to open that trick door for Miss Emma and the Chief, he'd had his bellyful of the Pronto Gang. Ain't that so, Cliff? You learned your lesson?'

'Throwin' in with 'em was the dumbest mistake of my life,' muttered Cliff.

'Suppose I don't turn you in – then what?' challenged Larry. 'Would you head on home with your sister, stay steady, forget about outlawin' and make a real cattleman of yourself?'

'I'd give all my teeth for that chance,' Cliff said fervently.

'Keep your teeth,' shrugged Larry.

'You'd – give me a break?' frowned Cliff.

'For your sister's sake,' nodded Larry. 'She's quality, the kind of lady that don't deserve a jailbird for a brother.' He drained his cup, got to his feet and moved to his pack for his field-glasses. 'You folks rest a while.'

'While you're doin' what?' asked Stretch.

'While I'm hopin' a law-posse's moseyin' around this high country,' said Larry. 'Cookfire smoke couldn't rise high enough for a scout to spot, but we had us quite a fire here today.'

'The brush burning,' observed Slow Wolf. 'And the inflammable liquid stored in the cabin. Yes, quite a fire.'

Cliff offered Larry his humble thanks and

directed him to the easy ascent once used by lookouts. Larry was gone almost an hour, during which time Emma's brother gave in to his curiosity. He could no longer stare at Slow Wolf and restrain his confusion; he had to be told.

'No offence, but what kind of an Injun are you anyway – what tribe?' he frowned.

'Up to you, Chief,' grinned Stretch. 'How much d'you want him to know?'

'This becomes tiresome,' complained Slow Wolf. 'Not to mention embarrassing.'

'Brother, all you need to know, and it's supposed to be a secret, is that our friend Slow Wolf had a most impressive education,' said Emma. 'He *is* our friend, and that's the important thing. So leave it at that. No more questions.'

Later, when Larry reappeared, Stretch noted, 'He looks happy about somethin'.'

'Not just my cooking?' asked Emma.

'An excellent repast, my dear Emma,' Slow Wolf declared. 'My compliments to our charming chef.'

Rejoining them, Larry announced with a broad grin, 'We ain't gonna have to fret about buryin' them bandidos nor where to take the dinero.'

'You spotted a posse,' guessed Stretch.

'Big'un, and headed thisaway,' reported Larry. 'But they got all that brush to get through, so we can take our time packin' up. Chief, you might's well open up again.'

Emma took her brother's horse from the corral, found his saddle and readied the animal for the trail. The loot was left where Slow Wolf had inspected it and gear re-secured to the pack-horse. The Texans reloaded and sheathed their rifles and, by the time the search-party from Alvarado ventured into the thick brush west, the victors were near ready to leave.

Keen-eyed Paiute Jake had sighted smoke, reason enough for Daniel P. Hoolahan to jump to conclusions and order his party to detour in that direction.

'This ain't the first posse I've rid with,' an Alvarado man remarked. 'And I never saw smoke like that before – risin' up out of a mountain.'

'From here, it looks like a volcano,' observed Zimmerman.

'My instincts tell me the Pronto Gang's getting careless,' said Hoolahan. 'One of those blackguards started a fire that couldn't be controlled – thus playing right into my hands.'

'Sometimes we call him Lucky Hoolahan,' Casey muttered to Deputy Falk.

'But not often,' said Zimmerman.

'Forward, men!' boomed Hoolahan.

'Look, Mister Detective, this is your expedition,' frowned Sheriff Breakstone. 'I don't mean to challenge your authority, but …'

'So *don't*!' warned Hoolahan.

' … but – damn and blast!' fumed Breakstone, as the horsemen began the difficult climb. 'We don't even have a trail to follow, so ease up for pity's sakes! This brush is gettin' thicker – could tear a man's eye out!'

'So much for dauntless county sheriffs,' jibed Hoolahan. He charged his mount forward and upward, forcing a branch to bend. It then swung back to strike his face and violently deprive him of his derby. He paused, cursing. 'Agent Casey! Retrieve my hat!'

'Where'd it go?' wondered Casey.

'I got it,' Falk called to them. He dismounted to rescue Hoolahan's tile, swung astride again and urged his horse up level with the boss-Pinkerton's. 'Here you go, Irish. Sorry about the damage. Looks like one of the horses trod on it – maybe a couple horses.'

Seething with impatience, well aware some possemen were grinning, Hoolahan snatched his worse-for-wear headgear from the deputy. The crown was badly dented. He used a fist to smooth the dents, but succeeded only in punching a large hole right through the crown. Casey hastily looked away. Zimmerman clamped hand to mouth to muzzle his mirth. Red-faced, Hoolahan redonned his derby; the ascent was resumed.

When, finally, the riders reached the flat ground at the mountain's near base, Falk at once spotted the gap and gaped incredulously.

'Holy Moses – will you look at *that*!'

'I'll be damned,' breathed Breakstone, dropping hand to holster. 'If I can believe my eyes – it's some kind of door – and it's open.'

'*Another* fatal mistake!' gloated Hoolahan. 'Not only did they show smoke. Some Pronto man left the secret entrance open!' He drew his pistol, manoeuvred his mount ahead of the sheriff's and, at the full strength of his lungs, yelled, '*Charge* ...!'

'Hold it,' growled Breakstone. 'Everybody stay quiet – and listen!'

'*I'm* in charge of ...!' blustered Hoolahan.

'I hear 'em too, Jeff,' muttered Falk, unsheathing his rifle.

'Horses,' said Breakstone. 'Some kind of passage beyond that opening – riders comin' out, but comin' slow. Cover the entrance, boys. Don't anybody open fire till I give the word.'

As they ambled their mounts into the tunnel, Stretch glanced sidelong at his partner.

'Ol' Hothead Hoolahan? You sure?'

'Had 'em all in close focus,' nodded Larry. 'Big party. Saw Dan'l real clear. You know, this'll break his heart.'

'What's the matter?' grinned Stretch. 'You feelin' ashamed?'

'I wouldn't go *that* far,' said Larry. Glimpsing horsemen beyond the entrance, he called to them curtly, 'Don't nobody get trigger-happy! No Pronto men comin' out! Just three law-abidin' hombres, a lady and an honest Injun!'

'Hey!' Casey nudged Zimmerman. 'That sounded like ...!'

'It *is* him!' chuckled Zimmerman.

Hoolahan's jaw sagged; his complexion changed from red to purple.

'No ...!' he raged. 'I refuse to believe ...!'

But then he had to believe his eyes. Through the opening, two familiar riders emerged, followed by a short-haired woman in male attire and a young man with his right arm in a makeshift sling. Last out was a portly redman forking a dun and leading a pack-horse.

Breakstone, like several hundred other lawmen, held a fat file on the famous outlaw-fighters complete with copies of newspaper photographs. Easily recognizing them, he ordered his men to put up their weapons.

Hoolahan was shocked speechless; this did happen on rare occasions. It was left to Breakstone to address the Texans. He identified himself and put his question, which the Texans conceded was fair and reasonable.

'Well, like you can see, we found the Pronto Gang's hideout,' offered Larry.

'Just like that?' blinked Falk.

'Ain't claimin' it was easy,' said Larry. 'You see, I had to try findin' 'em on account of a half-dozen of 'em kidnapped my partner, Mister Emerson here.'

'That's how it was, gents,' nodded Stretch. 'They spiked my booze in Kingsville and fetched me here. Seems their boss, a mean buzzard name of Jethro Tragg, toted an old grudge against me.'

'Along the way I met up with Miss Emma here and her brother,' continued Larry. 'Tragg and five of his gun-toters looted a bank in their hometown, Harperville, a while back, left a cashier dead. Just happens that cashier was a good friend of theirs, so they hankered to square accounts.'

'I've heard of Harper County,' said Breakstone. 'It's a long way north, young lady. You and your brother travelled all that distance with the idea of fightin' the whole Pronto Gang?'

Emma matched his stare without flinching.

'You heard,' she said. 'Go on, Larry, tell this lawman everything. We *have* come a long way, and it'll be just as long going back.'

'After Emma and Cliff and me kind of joined forces, we got lucky and ran into an old friend of ours,' said Larry, gesturing to Slow Wolf. 'Never did learn his real name. We just call him Chief. And this ain't the first time he's sided us.'

'We can always count on him,' said Stretch.

'If it wasn't for the Chief, we'd never've found this door and the tunnel,' Larry told Breakstone.

'It's camouflaged as you can see,' offered Emma. 'It took the keen eye of our peaceful Sioux friend to detect that transplanted brush had been used to conceal the door.'

'So that's all there is to tell,' said Larry. 'We got in, none of them bandidos'd surrender, so we had to fight 'em.' He jerked a thumb. 'You'll have to organize a burial detail, Sheriff. I wouldn't know how much loot Tragg saved from his cabin after we set it afire. You'll find what's left.'

'There were – how many in the gang?' frowned Falk.

'Thirteen, countin' the guard they always left here,' said Larry.

'That explains how they seemed to raid places far apart inside a few days,' muttered Breakstone. 'They divided their force. Two separate parties of six.'

'That's all we can tell you,' said Emma. 'And now, if you'll kindly let us pass, we have a long journey ahead of us.'

'Dan'l ol' buddy, you could use a new hat,' Stretch couldn't resist remarking, as he passed Hoolahan. 'Important gent like you, big shot Pinkerton and all, oughtn't wear a tile so toil-worn.'

'Damn you, Emerson, and you too, Valentine!' gasped Hoolahan.

'Nice seein' you again, Dan'l,' drawled Larry. He nodded affably to Casey and Zimmerman and, to Breakstone, declared, 'We're all through in there. Your bunch might's well take care of the buryin' and the horses and tallyin' the dinero.'

As they slowly made their way down through the brush to seek the trail, the victors discussed